The Summoning

Also by E. E. Richardson:

The Devil's Footsteps
The Intruders

E. E. RICHARDSON

The Summoning

CORGI

THE SUMMONING
A CORGI BOOK 978 0 552 55388 9

First published in Great Britain by The Bodley Head
an imprint of Random House Children's Books
A Random House Group Company

The Bodley Head edition published 2007
Corgi edition published 2008

1 3 5 7 9 10 8 6 4 2

The Random House Group Limited supports the Forest Stewardship Council (FSC),
the leading international forest certification organization. All our titles that are
printed on Greenpeace-approved FSC-certified paper carry the FSC logo.
Our paper procurement policy can be found at
www.rbooks.co.uk/environment

Mixed Sources
Product group from well-managed
forests and other controlled sources
www.fsc.org Cert no. TT-COC-2139
© 1996 Forest Stewardship Council
FSC

Corgi Books are published by Random House Children's Books,
61–63 Uxbridge Road, London W5 5SA

www.**kids**at**randomhouse**.co.uk
www.**rbooks**.co.uk

Addresses for companies within The Random House Group Limited can be found at:
www.randomhouse.co.uk/offices.htm

THE RANDOM HOUSE GROUP Limited Reg. No. 954009

A CIP catalogue record for this book is available from the British Library.

Printed in the UK by CPI Bookmarque, Croydon CR0 4TD

For K. C.

'Justin, I really don't think this is a good idea.' Trevor's voice had been growing steadily higher as he got more and more agitated. 'We'll never make it over there and back in time. And what if they ask to see our passes when we get back? Justin . . .'

'Trevor, relax.' Justin couldn't help but roll his eyes. 'It's not like we're *bunking*. How is it any of their business if we go out at lunch? We'll be back before last lesson. It's only geography, anyway. Who cares if we miss a few minutes?'

Nobody but Trevor. Justin had been friends with him since infant school, but even he had to admit that Trevor Somerville could be a wet blanket sometimes. It wasn't exactly his fault, he just *worried* – all the time, and about everything. He had panic attacks if he forgot to do his homework or bring his trainers for PE, never mind anything more daring. Justin was doing his best to teach him to live dangerously, but it was an uphill struggle.

'Couldn't we do this after school?' Trevor continued plaintively. 'Or at the weekend? We don't have to go today . . .'

'Yes we do.' Justin sighed in exasperation. 'I've got to get the key back before my parents get home, remember? My dad'll kill me if he knows I've been over to Grandpa's house while he's still in California.'

Not that his father would be any happier if he went there while Grandpa Blake was home. As far as Thomas Blake was concerned, his father was a crazy old man who needed to be stopped from filling the children's heads with weird ideas.

Which, of course, was exactly why Justin and his sister found him so interesting. After all, how many people could say they had a grandfather who studied the occult?

'I'm not sure this is such a good idea,' Trevor repeated miserably, already out of breath as he hurried to keep up with Justin's bike. He was really only a little bit overweight, but there was no telling him that; he was his own worst enemy, hiding in baggy clothes that made him look twice the size, and not even trying to exercise because he was too embarrassed.

In fact Trevor tried hard to avoid doing *anything* that was not part of his usual routine, which was why Justin had pushed so hard when he'd admitted to being interested in Grandpa Blake's strange hobbies. 'Hey, you were the one who said you wanted to see his collection,' Justin reminded him.

'Yeah, but you didn't say anything about sneaking out of school,' he protested.

'Look, this is the only chance we're going to get to do it. My dad doesn't like me and Joy going round there at all – and even when we do go, Grandpa Blake never lets us look at the cool stuff.'

Justin didn't really believe that the things his grandfather collected had mystical powers, but that didn't make them any less fascinating. There was one particular book his grandpa kept locked up: he'd only managed to take the quickest skim through it, but the contents had been jaw-dropping. A genuine book of magic! It almost didn't matter that the things in it had to be made up. It was cool just to imagine how many people had pored over its pages before him, prepared to do all sorts of strange and terrible things.

Trevor was still finding reasons to whine, but Justin tuned him out and pedalled faster. He'd been waiting for the chance to have a better look at that spellbook for ages. This was a golden opportunity, and he wasn't going to waste it.

'See, what did I tell you?' he said as he jumped off his bike outside Grandpa Blake's house. 'It's only just gone half one. We've got plenty of time. Now come on.' He unlocked the front door and they went inside.

Grandpa Blake had been gone only days, but the air inside already had a stale flavour. Letters and a newspaper were piled on the mat, and Justin stepped over them carefully.

Trevor hung back in the doorway. 'Maybe I should . . .'

'Oh, come *on*.' Justin groaned in disbelief. 'At least come in and see it.'

It was a collection, after all. Collections were meant to be looked at. It was only Dad who had stupid objections – if it was up to Grandpa, he surely wouldn't have minded Justin bringing a friend round.

Justin squashed the feeling of guilt that was trying to rear its head and led the way.

Grandpa Blake's private study was more like a back room in a museum than an office or a cosy den. The shelves were loaded with weird objects, from stone carvings to animal skulls to something that looked like a mummified hand. Instead of letters or reminder notes, the pinboard above the desk was covered with carefully inked drawings: star charts, odd anatomical diagrams and geometric patterns, often labelled in strange alphabets.

Compared to all that, the stacks of books were rather a let-down. They covered some interesting topics – witchcraft, Egyptian gods, fortune-telling – but they were, after all, just books. Some of them were pretty old, but most looked like you could

E. E. Richardson

have bought them in any high-street bookshop.

Justin had always suspected that in a room like this there should be . . . other books. And one day last year, when they'd dropped by a little earlier than Grandpa was expecting, he'd found what he was looking for.

Now he went to the cupboard in the corner of the room and hauled out the chest from the bottom of it. As he carried it over to the desk, he couldn't help but smile at the wide-eyed way Trevor was gazing around.

'All this stuff is actually *real*?' his friend asked in amazement.

Justin shrugged. 'Supposedly. And this' – he tapped the chest – 'is *definitely* the real deal.' He tried to tug it open, but wasn't surprised when the lid wouldn't budge.

'It's locked?' said Trevor, sounding disappointed.

'Yeah, it was last time. Don't worry, I know where he keeps the key.' Justin pulled out the desk drawer and was relieved to see the key in the tray full of odds and ends where he'd found it before. He was about to push it shut again when something at the back caught his eye. 'Oh, *wow*. Check this out.'

He reached in and withdrew a dagger in a hard scabbard, its blade about the length of his hand. The handle was made of something like brass or bronze, icy cold to the touch but still comfortable to hold. He faced away from Trevor as he drew it, certain even before he saw it that the blade would be wickedly sharp.

'Cool.' Trevor admired it as he held it up to the light. 'Is that supposed to be magical too?'

'It's got to be.' Justin sheathed the blade again and impulsively tucked it into his bag while Trevor wasn't looking. Then he knelt down and unlocked the chest.

'This is it.' He dug through the folds of pale blue material that lined the box and unveiled the book. Trevor leaned forward curiously.

This book bore no resemblance to even the oldest volumes up on the shelves. The dark leather binding was cracked with age and bore no author's name or title; the inside page read simply, *'An account of secrets gathered'*. The whole thing was handwritten, brownish ink on brittle, rough-textured paper.

It practically *exuded* hidden knowledge, as if you could absorb it through your fingertips just by having the thing in your hands.

'Wow,' Trevor breathed reverently, and Justin mentally echoed the sentiment.

He resisted the urge to flick through it, knowing that if he did, he'd never tear himself away. The day he'd first discovered it he'd almost been caught, and he'd spent every subsequent visit to his grandpa's just itching to get a second look.

And now it was his . . .

Justin quickly clamped the covers closed and stood, clearing his throat. 'OK. We'd better get back to school.'

Justin had told himself that he wouldn't even glance at the book until the school day was over, but it didn't take long for his resolution to fade. Geography was boring, and Mr Payne had made him and Trevor sit at separate desks because they'd come in late. Before the first ten minutes had passed, he'd eased the book out of his bag and opened it up on his lap.

When he'd first managed to find it, he hadn't had the time to get a real look at his prize: just a few tantalizing glimpses of cramped, spidery handwriting and disturbing images. Now that he could actually sit down and read it, he was disappointed to find that a lot of it wasn't even in English.

In fact it seemed to be written in a whole mess of different languages. Some, like Latin and German, he could at least vaguely recognize; others were completely alien, even the scribbled shapes of the letters unfamiliar. All the same, he found it hard to wrench his gaze away.

The brittle pages whispered as he turned them, and the air felt thick with secrets. He was sure that if he could only block the rest of the world out, shut himself away with the book and no distractions, then he would begin to understand.

Understand everything. Be able to *do* everything. Be all-powerful . . .

Justin turned another page and finally found a section that was written in English. A section that made the hairs on the backs of his arms stand up as he began to read.

'Oh, *wow*,' he breathed softly, completely forgetting about his surroundings.

The page was headed in sweeping calligraphic script with the words: *The Summoning and Binding of*

Major Spirits. Half the page was taken up by a complex circular design, with places marked out at points for four people to stand or sit. Below that, numbered with Roman numerals, were detailed directions and the words of ritual invocations.

The words of an actual spirit-raising ritual that people had once tried to do. How awesome was that?

It didn't even look like it was all that complicated. Chalk, candles, a few bits to read out . . . they could do it themselves. Justin smirked at the thought of what Trevor would say if he suggested it.

He was about to turn the page when a harsh ringing sound interrupted. It took a moment for him to realize that it was the end-of-school bell. Three thirty already? Where had the rest of the lesson gone? He hadn't even started the work.

Not that he really cared. Justin closed his untouched geography book. He glanced round and saw that Mr Payne had already left.

'Justin? Are you coming?'

'Yeah, in a minute.' He pushed past the waiting Trevor to get to the front of the class. They still had blackboards in the classrooms in this part of the school. Justin pocketed a stick of chalk from the shelf beneath.

'Justin!' Trevor looked alarmed.

'Don't worry, it's just *chalk*.' He held up his hands and rolled his eyes. 'It's not like it's a TV or anything.'

'What do you want chalk for?'

'I'll show you. I was looking through that book and I found this really cool— Hey!' As he turned back to his desk, Justin saw that the book was gone.

The book was gone because Daniel Eilersen had picked it up and was standing there casually leafing through it. Justin charged over, indignant. 'Hey, Eilersen! Get your thieving hands off! Did I say you could touch that?'

He snatched the book back and inspected it for damage.

Eilersen gave him a flat stare. 'Oh, right. I'm the one who's thieving. And that chalk just *fell* into your pocket, I'm sure.' He gave an exaggerated eye-roll that made Justin want to punch him. 'What do you think you're going to use that for? Don't tell me you actually expect to be able to cast spells. Where did you get the book from – Gullible Idiots dot com?'

Daniel Eilersen had always been the worst kind of know-it-all – the kind who thought everyone else was just dying to hear his opinion. He might be top of the class in everything, but even the teachers didn't like him. He was the sort of person who'd rather complain about the wording of the questions than answer them.

'For your *information*,' Justin said icily, 'it's a one-of-a-kind priceless artefact from my grandfather's occult collection. So you can keep your slimy hands off it.'

'Your grandfather? Wow. Stupidity really is down to genetics. The only reason people believe in magic,' Eilersen said pompously, 'is because they're too pathetic to cope with living in the real world. Why actually try and solve your problems when you can ask the pixies to take them away?'

'You just don't want to believe in anything you can't understand,' Justin accused.

'I believe in lots of things I don't understand. I believe in the theory of relativity. I believe in space travel. I believe in brain surgery. I believe in things that can be *scientifically proven*.' Eilersen folded his arms as if he'd already won the argument, which only made Justin twice as irritated.

'You want proof? Then come along and see us prove it,' he challenged. 'Me and Trevor are going to do one of these rituals tonight.' Trevor's eyes practically bugged out at that, but Justin shot him a warning glare to keep him quiet. 'You know the playground off Llewellyn Road? Meet us there at eight o'clock tonight and I'll show you some things from this book that will make you *wet yourself*.'

'From laughing?' Eilersen pretended to consider. 'Yes – you playing wizard probably *would* be that funny. What are you going to do, amaze me with your ability to make ping-pong balls disappear?'

'Oh, this isn't party tricks,' Justin said, holding his gaze. 'This is *real* magic. The kind where you'll get your head ripped off if you do it a fraction wrong. Ever seen someone summon a spirit?' He smiled nastily. 'Oh, wait – you don't believe in them. So I guess you won't be afraid to try it, then, will you?'

'Wow. What cunning use of psychology. What's

next – are you going to make chicken noises?'

'I don't need to.' Justin smirked. 'I know you. There's no *way* you can resist a chance to prove you're right and I'm wrong.' Eilersen's dark eyes narrowed fractionally behind his glasses, and Justin knew that he had him. 'Llewellyn Road park, eight o'clock. Be there. Come on, Trev.'

He scooped up his bag and led the way out of the classroom.

As soon as they were away from Eilersen, Trevor grabbed his arm. 'What was that for?' he moaned in dismay. 'You didn't say we were going to do magic. And why did you have to invite Eilersen? You know what he's like!'

'Exactly!' Justin laughed in triumph. 'He's always going around like he's so much smarter and cooler than everyone else. He's all, "You're so stupid if you believe that stuff," but I bet you anything he'll freak out if you actually make him test it. He'll be running home crying to his mummy before we get past the second line. It'll be awesome.'

'Yeah, but, Justin, that's a real book of magic,' Trevor said nervously. 'We shouldn't be messing around with that stuff! Who knows what it can do?'

Justin raised his eyes to the sky and sighed. 'It's not going to *do* anything, Trevor. It's just a load of words and lighting candles and crap. All this ceremonial magic stuff is just mind games. People get all psyched up and half hypnotized and they start seeing stuff that's not really there. And that's what we're going to do with Eilersen. I'm telling you, he'll lose his head.'

They'd reached the front of the school, and Justin paused to unlock his bike. 'Listen, I've got to get home,' he said. 'I've got to get this key back before my dad finds out I've got it. I'll see you there tonight, all right?'

He rode off without waiting for a reply.

Justin's mind whirred even faster than his pedals as he cycled, dodging cars and almost running down pedestrians. The ritual he'd looked at was meant for four people, but there was no reason why they couldn't fudge the details. It wasn't like they had to worry about it not working. He had the book, the ceremonial knife, the chalk he'd just grabbed . . . the only other thing he seemed to need was candles, and he was sure Dad had a load of them stored somewhere.

This was going to be *great*.

He threw his bike down in the garden without stopping to lock it up, and let himself in the front door. Dashing through to the kitchen, he rifled through the cupboard under the sink and pulled out a box of plain white candles. Perfect.

Now, what else did he have to do? The key. Put the key back, so his parents didn't know he'd been over to Grandpa's, and then he was truly home free. Justin pulled it out of his pocket and spun round to hang it on its hook.

'OK, what are *you* up to?' a voice demanded from the doorway to the dining room.

Justin jumped and then turned round to glare at his sister. 'Jesus, sneak up on me, why don't you?' he snapped.

'What were you doing at Grandpa's house?' she pressed, unapologetic.

At fourteen, Joy was less than a year and a half younger, and they sometimes got taken for twins. They both shared the same red-gold curly hair, but beyond that Joy looked a lot more like their mum: green eyes, rounded face and small nose, where Justin had the more striking Blake features. Yet somehow, right now, she managed to look *exactly* like Dad when he was waiting for an explanation.

Justin gave it his best shot. 'Just . . . checking on the house while he's away,' he said, hanging up the key with a short shrug.

'Yeah, right.' She snorted. 'What about the candles? "Just checking" in case we have a power cut?'

'I need them for school. Art project,' he said quickly.

'Oh, yeah? Let's see what else you've got here, then.' Joy swiped his school bag off the worktop before he had a chance to block her, and quickly uncovered the book. 'Oh-ho! Art project, is it?'

'Oi!' He made a grab to get it back, but his sister was too fast for him.

Joy flipped through a couple of pages. 'Dad is going to *kill* you,' she said incredulously. She peeked into the bag to see if there was anything else and discovered the knife. 'Justin!'

'What?' He threw out his hands in a shrug. 'I'm

just *borrowing* it!'

'To do what with? Have you ever listened to Grandpa Blake at all? This stuff is dangerous!'

Justin raised his eyebrows at her, smirking. 'Oh my *God*, you actually believe him.' He snickered. 'You believe in magic?'

'I believe you're an idiot,' she said defensively. 'What are you *doing* with all this stuff? If Dad catches you with it, he's going to think Grandpa Blake gave it to you. He'll probably never let us talk to him again!'

'He's not going to catch me,' he insisted. 'I've only got it for tonight. We're going to re-enact this spirit-summoning ritual and scare the crap out of Eilersen.' He couldn't help grinning in anticipation. 'It's going to be absolutely brilliant. You should come.' Then they'd have the full four people.

She snorted. 'Oh yeah, because I really care about your stupid feud with some kid in your class.'

'Hey, it's not just me!' Justin retorted. '*Everyone* hates him. He's such a know-it-all. I just want to see how fast he falls apart when he's actually face to face with the occult. He reckons he's so logical and rational, but I bet you anything he freaks out once the ritual starts. It'll be great.'

'Yeah. Great,' she said, very sarcastically. 'Don't know how I could miss that.'

'Oh, come on, Joy,' he wheedled. 'We could really do with a fourth person. And don't you want to see the ritual for yourself? This could be our chance to see once and for all whether Grandpa Blake's totally gaga, or if there's actually something to it.' He knew nothing would really happen, but Joy had always been more ready to believe in this stuff than he was.

'*You* don't believe in it,' she pointed out. Her arms were still folded stubbornly, but he knew she was wavering. Joy acted like she was the smart and sensible one, but he could always talk her into doing anything he wanted.

'Well, I haven't *seen* anything to make me believe in it, have I?' Justin said, shrugging. 'Think of this as our chance to give Grandpa the benefit of the doubt. Dad would never let him try to show us any magic, so we'll do a test for ourselves. It's only fair.'

She shook her head in disbelief, but then sighed. 'You're going to go ahead with this whatever I say,

21

aren't you?' she said resignedly.

'Hey, I can't back out now,' he reminded her. 'Family pride is at stake.'

Joy snorted rudely. 'Fine,' she said. 'I'll come. But *only* because I know you're bound to get yourself arrested or something if you do this without me.'

'Yeah, yeah, whatever,' Justin said, patting her on the shoulder. As he turned away, he was smiling.

So now there were four of them. They could do the whole ritual exactly as it was written in the book, and Eilersen would have to sit there shaking in his shoes, waiting to see if a spirit creature really did show up.

Oh, there was no doubting it. This was going to be *great*.

III

Trevor was waiting in front of the park gates, looking awkward and highly conspicuous. He almost collapsed in relief as the two of them rode up. 'I was worried you weren't going to come.'

'Hey, like I was going to let Eilersen off that easily?' Justin jumped down from his bike and chained it to the railings. 'Assuming he's even going to show.'

'Let's hope he doesn't, and then we can all go home,' Joy muttered as she chained her bike alongside his. She was keeping up the act of being here under protest, but Justin wasn't fooled. She'd been dying to get her hands on the book all evening. He wasn't about to let her. This was *his* show, and he wasn't going to have his baby sister muscle in on it.

Even though he knew the ritual was bogus, there was a buzz of excitement in his stomach that refused to fade away. All the rational thinking in the world couldn't quite drown out the little voice that whispered, 'Yeah, but *what if . . .* ?'

What if it really *did* work?

'Oh. You're actually here.' The flat words coming out of the darkness made them all jump.

Eilersen stepped up into the glow cast by the street-light, as unnaturally neat as ever. Under his long coat, his crisp white shirt was buttoned right up to the collar, like he didn't want to expose even the tiniest sliver of skin. Even his jeans looked like they'd been carefully ironed and pressed.

'Ah, Danny-boy – you're a little late,' Justin noted. 'Almost lost your nerve?'

'Almost lost my will to live,' Eilersen said. 'I realized I was voluntarily spending an evening with you and I just couldn't make myself walk out of the door.'

Joy snickered, and Justin glared at her accusingly.

'OK,' he said sharply. 'Last chance for anybody to back out.'

There was silence, until finally his sister said, 'Just get *on* with it, Justin. It's freezing.'

'All right!' Irritated, he turned away and pushed through the park gates, always unlocked after long-ago vandalism that no one had bothered to fix. Already he was regretting bringing his sister in. He could rely on Trevor to follow his lead, but Joy was going to ruin everything if she kept breaking the atmosphere. Did she miss the memo about the point being to *frighten* Eilersen?

He calmed down a little as he led the way past the shadowed swings and climbing frame to the old tennis courts. The nets were long gone and so was most of the fencing that had once surrounded them, but the patch of flat ground would do for their purposes. It was nearly pitch-black here, the house windows and streetlights too far away to spill any light on them.

'It's a little bit dark for reading, don't you think?' Eilersen said, as if they were too stupid to have thought of that.

Justin took advantage of the darkness to make a

few hand gestures. 'Yeah, I've *got* candles,' he said in his best 'duh' tone. He fumbled one out of his bag and managed to get it lit. The pool of light it gave was smaller than he expected, and the heat and the smell both much stronger. It was a different kind of light to the neutral glow of a torch-bulb, raw and unreliable. When he opened up the book, the ink seemed to glisten like blood.

'Is that the ritual?' Trevor leaned forward, half anxious, half fascinated.

Justin nodded. 'That's it.' His own voice sounded hoarse, like he had a sore throat

'Let me see.' Eilersen lifted the book into his lap and scanned the pages, pulling a series of steadily more disbelieving faces. He rolled his eyes dramatically as he handed it back. 'Well, go on, then,' he said. 'Wow me with your incredible mastery of the dark arts.'

Justin narrowed his eyes, but bit back a million possible comments. He was sure that smug front would shatter once the ritual was properly underway.

Assuming it ever got that far. For someone who kept insisting that magic was nonsense, Eilersen was infuriatingly pedantic about getting the details right.

Justin had barely started chalking the magic circle when the nit-picking began.

'It doesn't *matter*, Eilersen,' Justin growled at him, after the third time his lines were criticized for being a millimetre off.

'So you *say*. But if this is an experiment, then we're doing it exactly by the book. No leaving room to pretend it only failed because you did it wrong.'

'Gah.' Justin sat back and exchanged a long-suffering look with his sister. 'Fine. *You* do the drawing.' He tossed the stick of chalk across to land in Eilersen's lap.

Eilersen's idea of 'doing it by the book' involved ridiculously precise measurements, sketching guidelines and generally taking about fifteen times as long as any normal person. When he started making careful little tick-marks round the circle to get the points of his star spaced *just* right, Justin groaned and put his head down on the ground.

It was at least an hour later and several degrees colder when the circle was finally finished. Most of Justin's body had gone numb from the chill, and Joy had zoned out entirely, spinning the sheathed dagger round and round and staring at the patterns it made in the candlelight. Only Trevor had been watching avidly – feeding Eilersen's delusion that other people were only there to fawn over him.

Justin had to admit grudgingly that it was a magnificent circle. Annoying as he was, Eilersen *did* have a huge amount of patience, and the chalked design on the ground was a perfect replica of the one shown in the book. It was made up of simple shapes, but there were so many of them overlaid one on the other that it ended up looking quite intricate. At various points there were runes and strange symbols, although there was no explanation of what they were supposed to do or represent.

Joy and Trevor lit a fresh group of candles and placed them at points around the circle. Once their original light was blown out, the four of them were forced to huddle closer, gathering around the circle in order to see. Justin kept looking down nervously to check he wasn't edging over the chalk lines. Not that he really believed the book's warnings about spirits getting free to wreak havoc, of course. He just didn't want to mess it up and have Eilersen decide to draw it all again.

He consulted the book. 'We need to be kneeling. Make sure you're lined up with the candles.' Eilersen had made a great production of aligning the whole thing using the compass on his wrist-watch, after all. Justin took his position at the northernmost, Trevor sitting on his right and Eilersen on his left.

'OK. Now, when I pass you the book, you need to pull out a strand of your hair and then burn it over the candle flame while you say the words.'

The book actually said to offer 'a hair, a nail, a tooth, or blood', but he suspected he could only push the others so far. His sister was glowering at him as it was.

'You what?'

'Just do it, OK, Joy?' he said impatiently. 'I'll pass the book round when I've read the beginning bit.'

Justin looked down at the pages and felt the skin at the back of his neck begin to prickle. He'd read and rehearsed the words again and again earlier that evening, but somehow out here in the dark they took on a new power.

'Spirits of the world beyond, take heed!' His voice unexpectedly wobbled, and he cleared his throat quickly to hide it. 'Take heed!' he repeated. 'Come, all spirits, from the East, South, West and North, and let the strongest among you answer my call.'

He passed the book to Eilersen, who very precisely pulled out a single hair and held it over the flame. 'I evoke and conjure thee, Spirit, by the element of air, and by my own mind,' he recited, face expressionless.

Joy rolled her eyes, but obediently plucked out a long, near-invisible strand of hair. 'I evoke and conjure thee, Spirit, by the element of fire, and by my own heart,' she muttered perfunctorily before handing the book on.

Trevor gabbled his line a bit too fast, obviously nervous. 'I evoke and conjure thee, Spirit, by the element of water, and by my own will.' He snatched his fingers back hastily, as if afraid of scorching them.

The book was passed back to Justin, and he took a deep breath. 'I evoke and conjure thee, Spirit, by the element of earth, and by my own hand.'

Then, before any of the others could move to stop him, he raised the bronze-handled knife and sliced the blade across his left palm.

'Justin!' his sister yelled in alarm, and Trevor let

out a startled squeak. Justin ignored them and held his bleeding hand out over the flickering flame. He couldn't tell in the dark if the blood was even dripping, but it was the gesture that mattered. Both for the benefit of the others watching . . . and because blood would make the ritual stronger. Much stronger than just using hair.

Was that something he'd learned from his grandfather, or knowledge that just came instinctively? He couldn't quite seem to think straight. The words of the spell were bubbling up in his brain, as if the book intended to spill its contents with or without his help. He found himself beginning to speak, bold and sure despite the tremor that shook his upraised hand.

'Come, Spirit, and show thyself within the circle! By our sacrifice we call thee; by our will and strength of heart be bound. Come, and seek not to deceive or to harm those who summon thee. Show thyself in fair and visible form, and make clear and rational answers to our questions. So I command!'

The words in English bled on into collections of guttural syllables, no language Justin had ever heard, and yet somehow he didn't falter or stumble. His own voice sounded like a stranger's to him, deeper, stronger, more precise. He could feel the power rippling under his skin, like electricity waiting to leap.

He raised his head and roared the final incantation. 'By these words, I call thee present; by these words, I hold thee bound. Spirit, I command thee, appear!'

His words were matched by an enormous *crack* like a bolt of lightning, and the candle flames bent outwards, as if a wind was blowing from the centre in all directions at once. Blue-black smoke funnelled together over their heads, billowed . . . and expanded.

It was as if the smoke was pouring into an invisible mould, filling out the shape of a human head and torso. It was the body of a boy, perhaps their age, but impossibly handsome – so flawless, in fact, it was almost repulsive, too perfect to be real. Inhuman, like a computer simulation of a person, or an expensive shop-window mannequin.

The threads of smoke gradually solidified, until they were looking at something like a statue of living marble. Only . . . not, Justin realized, a chill scraping down his spine. It might be moving, but that didn't make it *alive*. This was . . . something else. Something alien and terrible.

Its eyes were far blacker than the night sky behind it, and so cold he forgot how to breathe.

The spirit smiled, an expression glittering with malice. 'So, you conjure me . . . and I appear.' Its voice was a mimicry of Justin's, but so loaded with ugliness that he almost didn't recognize it. 'Tell me, what is your command, O *Master*?'

The sarcasm in the address was unmistakable.

Joy's legs had gone numb quite some time ago; now it felt like her insides had joined them. Her brain seemed to have melted into a puddle of ice-water that was now seeping down her spine, leaving her unable to think or breathe or do anything but stare.

The thing in the circle was completely focused on Justin, and for that she felt a shameful stab of gratitude. Just sitting this close to it was like having maggots squirming all over her skin; if it turned and looked at her, she didn't know what she would do. She wanted to scream at her brother to stop this before it spun even further out of control, but she couldn't even open her mouth.

And she wasn't sure Justin would listen. His face had gone so white it was colourless even by candle-light, but beneath the shock she saw the awe and triumph.

The boys to either side of her had gone rigid with terror; she could hear Trevor hyperventilating, possibly even sobbing, and a choked-off sound from Eilersen that might have been a swearword. She didn't dare turn away for long enough to get a good look at either of them. She wasn't sure her muscles would have obeyed her if she'd tried.

Justin's head bobbed as he swallowed nervously. 'You – er, thou art bound by the ritual to obey my command,' he faltered, the hesitation making it sound more like a question.

'You believe I answer to *you*?' the spirit said contemptuously. 'Your magic is painfully weak, and you are a poorly taught child. Even the language you use is beyond your understanding.'

Perversely, that was what it took to make Justin straighten up and grow bolder. 'Silence, Spirit!' he snapped, for a second sounding just like his grand-father. 'You're bound to obey me, no matter how I speak.'

The spirit inclined its head a fraction of a millimetre – maybe an acknowledgement, maybe just a shift of position. There was nothing remotely submissive about the gesture.

Joy licked her dry lips, risking a quick glance down to check on the magic circle. The lines glowed, a brilliant electric blue that was painful to look at. She shivered with the thought that all that protected them now was Eilersen's precision. If Justin had been the one to draw it, with his usual slapdash impatience . . .

She stole a sideways glance at Eilersen, but she couldn't tell from his rigid face if he was still frozen with fear or if he had got his emotions back under control. She really hoped it was the latter, because nobody else here looked like they were on top of things. Trevor was still panting as if he was one sudden noise away from a heart attack, and Justin . . .

There was a light in her brother's eyes, and it was more than the reflected glow of their enchantments. In her mind's eye, Joy saw the way he'd sliced his own hand open, and her insides squirmed. What had he been *thinking*?

What was he thinking now? She had no idea how far he planned to take this, and that was almost as frightening as what they'd managed to do already.

'What is your name, Spirit?' Justin demanded, jaw set with determination.

The spirit let loose a mocking chuckle. 'Do you know nothing at all, little wizard? You cannot command *that* of me. Some have called me Dracherion; you may use that name if you wish. What you call me means nothing. Only true names have true power . . . and I know yours, Justin Lucien Blake. You bear your grandfather's name, but it seems you are even more foolish.'

Justin flinched, but quickly covered it. 'I didn't ask you to speak about him.'

'Then what *do* you ask, little wizard?' it taunted.

'Justin—' Joy finally found her voice – only to lose it again as Dracherion swivelled round to face her.

On the surface, the spirit's face was boyish and stunningly beautiful, with skin smooth as that of a statue. The smile, if you captured it in a sketch of the moment, would be charming and gentle.

A pencil sketch couldn't catch the waves of malev-
olence that were coming off the thing like radiation.
She was sure it wanted her dead; it wanted them all
dead. It was a being that would destroy the entire
universe if it could, and they had it trapped in a cage
of light and chalk that was as thin as a spider's web.

She choked.

'Ah, the baby sister. How *sweet*,' it said with a leer.
'And how convenient. The last of the Blake line
together, in one easily crushed package. And what
else do we have here?' It turned on Eilersen, and the
tone became sickeningly gleeful. 'A scientist! How
delightful. How does it feel, little scientist, to learn
that the universe obeys no rules?'

Eilersen swallowed hard. 'There must *be* rules, even
if we don't know them,' he said, managing to sound
almost steady even though he looked like he was
going to be sick. His eyes were huge behind his
glasses, and there was a noticeable tremor to his
shoulders.

Dracherion laughed, a deep, chilling cackle. 'Of
course,' it said, empty eyes narrowing down to slits.
'You would damn yourself and all around you before

you ever admitted that you could be wrong.' It wheeled round to face Trevor. 'And you – why are *you* here? Do you think you have something to contribute? You are *nothing*, and everyone here knows it.'

Trevor let out a strangled noise and squeezed his eyes shut tightly, as if that might be enough to make the spirit disappear.

'That's enough!' Justin commanded abruptly. He sat up and spoke with a precision that suggested he'd been rehearsing his words. 'Spirit, I command you to tell us what powers you have that can be used from inside the circle, without us being harmed or having to promise you anything.'

Joy shifted uncomfortably on the hard ground. It *sounded* like he was covering the loopholes, but she couldn't feel reassured. It seemed to her that trying to pin down Dracherion was like nailing droplets of water.

The spirit's eyes glittered. 'I can give knowledge,' it said, 'of hidden things and truths concealed. I can command all beasts and alter weather. I can tell of all those who think and speak of you at any given time. I can point to hidden treasures—'

'Stop,' said Justin abruptly, and Joy saw that his nervous grimace was spreading into a smile. 'I command you . . . to make it *snow*.' He gestured expansively, pleased with himself.

'As you wish.' Dracherion's words were curt and cool.

For a long time nothing seemed to happen. They were all tense as bow-strings. Eilersen twice made sharp, quickly aborted movements, as if he'd been about to speak and then changed his mind. His lips were pressed together in a tight, thin line that took the colour out of them.

Joy was on the verge of breaking the silence herself, but then she looked up.

The sky was growing lighter. As she watched, a solitary snowflake began drifting down towards them. Justin made as if to reach out and catch it, then flinched and quickly jerked his hand back. If he hadn't stopped himself, he would have been leaning into the circle.

Joy didn't know exactly what would happen if he did, but she had visions of arms stuck through bars into animal cages, electricity leaping when you bridged

E. E. Richardson

a gap with something that was a good conductor. The chalked circle was all that kept Dracherion imprisoned and under their power. If one of them edged just a fraction too far past the line . . .

It was a jarring reminder of the risks they were taking, and yet somehow, impossibly, Joy was starting to relax. After all, they were well aware they had to be on their guard. They *knew* that the spirit was going to try to trick them, and they were prepared for it. They were the ones in control here. And . . .

And it was *snowing*. Snowing, out of a sky that had been empty seconds earlier. Already the flakes were settling, coating the tennis courts and the park around them far faster than any normal blizzard.

They'd done this. The four of them, nobody else. They could control the *weather*.

What else could Dracherion do?

She heard Justin laugh and looked across to see him catching snowflakes on his tongue. Trevor was smiling nervously, and even Eilersen had relaxed out of his previous tension, staring at the sky in wonder as snow floated down onto his glasses.

The whole world was a blanket of white, snow

settling on the trees, the road outside, the roofs of houses. How far did it extend? Across the whole town? The whole country? And they could make it stop as easily as it had started, turn it into a sandstorm or torrential rain or anything they wanted . . .

Justin flashed her a grin across the circle. 'Go on, Joy. Your turn to ask something.'

She knew she ought to refuse and tell her brother to call an end to the ritual. They'd had their taste of genuine magic – pushing it further now was just asking for trouble. But then, looking up at the swirling snow, she thought of her silver necklace.

It had been a gift from Grandpa Blake, when she was about seven. He'd told her parents that the design was a snowflake, but then secretly told her that it was really a net to catch evil influences. She'd shrugged that off rather uncomfortably, as she always did Grandpa's strange comments, but she'd still worn the necklace almost every day – until one day it had simply vanished.

'You can find hidden things?' she asked the spirit, in a nervous rush. 'What about lost things?'

Dracherion nodded. Its gaze was cruelly amused,

but she sternly reminded herself that it was trapped, a slave to the circle. It couldn't do anything unless they let it.

'Tell me what happened to the silver snowflake necklace I lost,' she commanded, trying to sound like she believed her own authority.

The spirit's mocking smirk told her that she'd failed, but still, it inclined its head. 'The necklace you seek is in a drawer of the workbench in your parents' garage.'

Joy beamed in amazement. '*Really?* I thought it was stolen for sure.'

That almost made this whole crazy night worth it. But even so . . . 'Justin, we should end this soon,' she warned.

'Yeah, in a minute,' he said, waving her into silence. He gave Trevor an encouraging nudge. 'Go on, Trev, you ask it something.'

Trevor blanched, then ducked down and mutely shook his head.

Dracherion smiled, scenting fear. 'Nothing to ask?' it taunted. 'Nothing at all? No wonder they all hold you in such contempt. You resent your lack of power, yet you cower away when you find it freely offered.'

'That's enough.' Justin jumped in again, before it could spill even more venomous words. 'Eilersen, if you've got something to ask, make it quick,' he suggested brusquely.

Eilersen hunched closer to the circle, his head bowed down now to keep the worst of the snow off his glasses. 'I have a question,' he said quietly. 'What's to stop you harming us once this ritual is over?' His voice sounded calm, but his wide eyes betrayed him.

Dracherion smirked. 'The success of the banishment ritual you perform . . . nothing more.' Justin visibly gulped at that.

'Where will you go once you're banished?' Eilersen continued doggedly.

'Back into nothingness.' The words were spoken mildly, but there was a snarl behind them.

'And can you come back to . . . here, from nothingness?' Eilersen pushed his glasses further up on his nose, the careful gesture such a contrast to his snow-drenched appearance that Joy fought the urge to giggle. Hysteria beckoned if she did; she could *feel* things on the verge of tipping into disaster, like a boulder balanced at the top of a cliff. A wrong move, even an ill-timed breath, and it would all come to pieces around them.

'Only when I am called,' Dracherion said. 'Your ritual anchors me temporarily – a greater sacrifice is required if I am to remain.'

'So if you got out of the circle, you couldn't exist in our world.' Eilersen was clearly trying to get a grip on the new set of rules that had smashed all his old ones to pieces.

'I have no physical form in your world.' The spirit sneered at them. 'Unless, of course, I *take* one, from a mortal too weak to control it. And you have *bound* yourselves to me, foolish children – do you think the ties of blood magic go only one way?'

The candle flames abruptly flared and burned blood-red, and Dracherion's form swelled until it towered above them. Wreathed in dark smoke, the handsome human shape was twisting into something huge and grotesque, something that was not quite fully defined but had wings and horns and a tail . . .

Justin swore and fumbled frantically with the spell-book.

'It's *trying* to rattle you, Blake,' Eilersen said tightly.

'I *know* that!' That didn't mean it wasn't doing a good job of it.

'Justin,' Trevor said desperately, tugging at his sleeve.

'Not *now*, Trevor!' Justin snapped, throwing him off almost violently. He was riffling through the book at such a speed, Joy was afraid the brittle paper would disintegrate in his hands. The unnatural snow was still falling, but the sky had gone charcoal dark again. Dracherion glowed with its own inner light, a rusty blood-red like the candles, and it was still growing larger and larger . . .

'Justin!' Trevor shouted again, and yanked at him hard enough to almost pull him over. 'Just look at the circle! Look at the *circle*, Justin!' he blurted hysterically.

Tearing her eyes away from the spectacle of Dracherion, Joy looked down. The snow had been falling everywhere but inside the circle itself, but it had been piling up in the gaps between their bodies at an impossible rate. The drifts were getting taller and taller, and the wind was beginning to drive the heaped-up snow to encroach on one edge of the design.

Smearing the underlying chalk away.

Justin went as white as the snow that had settled on his hair, and his hands trembled visibly as he finally found the page he was looking for and began to read.

'I hereby license thee to depart, Spirit, and go in peace to the realm from whence thou came,' he gabbled, and now he only sounded like Justin, anxious and frightened and not at all like the deep-voiced stranger that had seemed to take him over during the ritual before. 'I conjure thee to withdraw peaceably from this place and harm none in departing, and seek not to return here until such time as I should call upon thee again. I hereby dismiss thee, and compel thee to obedience by the power—'

'What *power*?' The spirit's voice lashed out at a deafening volume, and the candles all snuffed out as one. The lines of the magic circle had dulled to a darker blue, as if they'd been lit by a battery that was now beginning to die. 'Your worthless little circle, carefully copied without the slightest knowledge of its meaning? The words that you read from a book without believing them? You *have* no power, worthless child, and yet you still dare to think you control me?'

Justin scrambled to his feet. 'I do!' he shouted desperately. 'It doesn't matter how powerful you are. While you're still in the circle, you can't hurt us.'

The spirit shrank down to its original boyish form so it was face to face with Justin. 'That is true,' it admitted gravely.

And then, in a flash that wasn't so much light as a sudden flare of darkness, it was out of the circle and *behind* him, close enough to have been touching if it had been solid.

'Unless, of course, the circle is already *broken*,' it whispered, millimetres from his ear.

The spirit's hand, hovering over Justin's shoulder, developed dark and terrible claws. They clenched, and Joy saw them go straight *through* Justin's flesh, as if he wasn't even there. Her brother's eyes rolled back in his head and he slumped to the ground.

'Justin!'

She jumped to her feet, but before she could run towards him, the spirit appeared between them. The face of its human form melted like wax, the neutral features shifting and re-forming into a copy of Justin's.

Only not quite. It was Justin's face, but smoothed and polished, stripped of all its flaws and asymmetry. Stripped of everything that made it human. The eyes that locked on Joy, unblinking, were not cornflower blue, but pure black right to the edges.

Dracherion smiled. It wasn't Justin's smile.

'You called, little girl?' the spirit taunted her. 'Want big brother to make it all better?'

It casually trailed its fingers across her chin, and she flinched backwards violently. There was no sensation of contact, but a tingling, spreading numbness, like a cold so intense it had burned away all feeling. If it had continued for much longer, she was sure she would have lost all control of her body and collapsed just like Justin.

'Your brother's magic is nothing.' Dracherion glanced back at the dimly glowing circle and blew a casual kiss down towards it. The light immediately winked out. 'The most feeble of enchanters would know better than to bind his fate to mine as you have all done. With every drop of blood each of you sheds, with every moment that you suffer, I will grow stronger. Soon I will take one of your bodies to wear

52

as my own, and then' – it smiled horribly – 'there will be no further need for the rest of you. Enjoy your last days well.'

It disappeared, and the park was plunged into darkness. Joy heard Trevor yelp in surprise.

She stood still for a long moment, her heart rattling in her chest and her breathing ragged. It took a while for her eyesight to adjust. The sky was actually quite bright, although she was sure it must be the middle of the night by now. It was still snowing.

With a jolt she remembered Justin and ran to where he'd fallen. He was just beginning to sit up and let out a heartfelt groan as she bent to help him.

'Are you all right?'

He touched his head gingerly. 'Er . . . yeah, I think . . .' He patted the ground around him and eventually found the knife, slipping it into his pocket as he stood. 'Crap – where's the book?'

'I've got it,' came a voice out of the darkness to her left.

Justin squinted. 'Eilersen?'

There was a scratch and brief flare of light ahead of them as Trevor shakily lit a match. 'Sorry. I couldn't find the other candles. Sorry,' he mumbled. 'I, er, can we – is it safe to go?'

'I don't know,' Joy said dazedly. She was shivering uncontrollably, and it wasn't just from the cold and wet.

'OK, what just happened here?' Eilersen said, somewhat unsteadily. 'Blake, did you *know* that was going to—?'

'Of course I didn't bloody— You think I expected that to *work*?' Justin demanded incredulously.

'It was your book! You said—'

'It was a *joke*, all right? I didn't think it would— It wasn't supposed to . . .' He trailed off, speechless.

Joy was distantly aware that she should probably be screaming or something, but somehow it all seemed very far away and small.

Trevor was looking all around in jerky motions, eyes flicking everywhere. 'So, that thing's, um . . . it's loose now?' he stuttered fearfully. 'It's just . . . flying around our world somewhere? Anywhere?'

'We didn't banish it,' said Eilersen. 'If we didn't banish it, then it hasn't gone back where it came from. And it *was* trapped in the circle, but then that got broken, so – so, I don't know!' he said despairingly.

He turned viciously on Justin. 'For Christ's sake, Blake! What were you thinking?'

'I was thinking that *it wouldn't do anything*!' Justin yelled back.

'Jesus! You two!' Joy choked out. She couldn't believe they were still fighting.

'It said "no need for the rest of us",' Trevor suddenly blurted, still twitching and staring every which way. 'What did it mean, "no further need for the rest of us"? Justin—'

'That was a threat, you *moron*.' Eilersen wheeled round to snap at him. 'It wants to possess one of our bodies, and then there'll be no need to keep the rest of us. As in, it can do anything it wants after that. Like, oh, I don't know, torture, maim, kill, destroy—'

'All right, give it a rest! We get the idea, thank you.' Snarling at Eilersen actually seemed to be helping Justin calm down a little. 'All right. Everybody just shut up a minute and let me think.'

He thought and then clicked his fingers triumphantly. 'Constanzo Coffee! They'll still be open even this late. We'll go there, we'll think of a plan and we will *fix* this,' he said decisively.

Joy wanted to believe him. She just couldn't for the life of her see how.

She checked her watch as they walked and was stunned to find that it wasn't yet quite ten o'clock. It seemed so impossible that she switched on her phone to confirm it. How could so much have happened in so little time? It felt like it should be at least three in the morning.

Joy turned the phone off again as she put it away. They'd been due home a while ago, but she just couldn't imagine trying to deal with angry parents right now. How could she make up lies about what they'd been doing when the terrible truth was hanging over her?

The snow was still coming down heavily, and they all trudged along in grim, shell-shocked silence. Justin was clutching hold of the book as if it was a lifeline.

'The answer's got to be in here,' he insisted, once they'd taken a window table in the coffee shop. 'All we've got to do is find another spell that'll send that thing back to the spirit world.'

'*All?*' Eilersen demanded disbelievingly. He spun

the book over to his own side of the table so he could look at it.

'Hey!' Justin reached across with his left hand to grab it back, then stopped and swore. He studied his palm and flexed it gingerly.

'Is it still bleeding?' Trevor asked anxiously.

Justin cautiously prodded the wound. 'No, it just . . . *ow*.'

'What the hell was that, anyway?' Joy demanded. 'You don't think the ritual's even real, but you still decide to take a knife and cut your *hand* open?'

'It's not deep!' he said defensively, like that made some kind of difference. 'The book said you could use blood as well as hair – I was just trying to make it look good! I didn't know it was going to *work*.'

'Oh, well, that makes it all better, then,' Eilersen sniped. He shut the book and pulled off his glasses, rubbing the bridge of his nose as if he had a brutal headache. 'This book is *impossible*. What, did you pick out the one page in the whole thing that's actually readable?'

'It's a book of magic! You were expecting what, *The Idiot's Guide to Spirit-raising*?' Justin demanded.

'I was expecting sentences to start and end in the same language!'

'Keep it down,' Trevor begged, shooting worried glances at the serving staff. 'They'll hear you.'

Eilersen ignored him. 'It could take *days* to search through this book for anything helpful. And I don't think that thing – Dracherion, or whatever it calls itself – is going to sit around and wait for us to finish. You've got to let me take this home with me.'

'Say what?' Justin yelped indignantly. 'Forget it! Why should I give it to you?'

'Because I'm bound to understand more of it than you are.' He didn't even speak as if he was bragging, but as if his superior knowledge was a widely accepted fact that no one could disagree with.

'Look, you utter—'

Whatever Justin was about to call him was interrupted by one of the coffee-shop staff. 'Sorry, kids, we're closing. I know it's still snowing, but you can't stay here all night.'

The snow had slackened off a little while they were inside, but the drifts were already knee-deep.

Joy, the shortest of the group by some margin, had trouble lifting her feet to wade through it.

'What's everybody going to think when they see all this snow?' Trevor wondered nervously.

'I don't know, but they're not going to think *we* did it, are they?' Justin growled. He was swaying, nearly asleep on his feet.

'Lucky you, off scot-free. Until we all *die*,' said Eilersen.

'Nobody's going to die,' Justin said irritably. '*Or* end up possessed. We'll find the answer. There's got to be something else in the book. Which I am not letting out of my sight, so forget it, OK?'

Eilersen glowered. 'After what happened back there, I wouldn't trust you to read the instructions on the back of a box of cornflakes. Give me the book.'

'Why don't you come back with us?' Joy interrupted, fairly sure her brother's next words weren't going to be helpful. 'That way you can *both* look at the book.'

That earned her equally incredulous looks from both boys.

'It's nearly eleven o'clock at night,' Eilersen protested.

'Yeah, Joy, it's just a *bit* late for visitors,' Justin pointed out.

Joy shrugged. 'So he can stay over.' Was this really the time to get bogged down in squabbling? 'You have people round overnight all the time.'

'Yeah, people I *like*,' her brother said sharply.

'Um, *no*, thank you,' Eilersen said at the same time. Which was enough to immediately provoke Justin into a U-turn.

'Oh, what, so you're supposed to be the only one smart enough to save us, but you won't do it if it puts you out at all?' He folded his arms. 'If you're so indispensable, then you'll have to come over. Otherwise you can shut up and sod off. Your decision.'

Eilersen's face went through a series of contortions, as if he was trying to swallow an extra-sour gobstopper.

'Fine,' he said eventually, and held out a hand. 'Somebody give me a phone.'

Trevor peeled off from them at the end of Hewlett Road, looking decidedly anxious to be the only one going home alone. Joy couldn't blame him, but it was pushing their luck to turn up with one uninvited guest, let alone two. Her parents knew Mrs Somerville, and could easily check up on any lie they told about why Trevor needed to stay.

Joy wasn't sure that numbers would give them any more security anyway. What could they possibly do if Dracherion came after them? She could only hope the spirit was as drained of energy as they were and wouldn't try anything more tonight.

Their father was waiting for them in the hallway when they got indoors. He looked stern, and for an irrational moment Joy was sure he knew exactly what they'd done. But all he did was fold his arms and say, 'Let me guess. You got caught in the snow?'

'We thought it would be best to wait for it to ease off a bit,' Justin said. Joy couldn't believe how easily he slipped into acting innocent.

'Uh-huh,' their dad said sceptically. 'And I suppose you conveniently forgot to have your phones switched on as well? It didn't occur to you to call home – or that *we* might be trying to call you?'

Justin smiled sheepishly, as if a missed phone call was truly the worst thing on his conscience. 'Sorry, Dad. We didn't think.'

'You never do, Justin, do you?' Their father sighed. No doubt they were only spared a longer lecture because he'd spotted Eilersen. 'Did you tell your mother you were bringing a guest back?' he asked, by which he meant, 'I already know you didn't.'

'Oh, er, this is . . . Daniel Eilersen. He got caught out in the snowstorm and he couldn't get home, so I said it would be OK if—'

The ringing phone interrupted Justin's rambling explanation. Dad frowned and moved to answer it, pausing in the doorway to give them a meaningful look.

'Take a moment to think what I'd be imagining right now if you hadn't just walked in the door,' he said bluntly. 'You didn't come home, you didn't call, I couldn't get through on your phones . . . you could have been dead or in jail for all I knew. Next time, if you really can't get home, for God's sake *let us know.*'

'Sorry, Dad,' Joy said miserably.

They really could have been dead. All of a sudden the doom Dracherion had laid on them felt sickeningly real. What awaited them if they couldn't find a way to fix this? Possession, or whatever terrible fate the spirit dreamed up for the three of them it considered worthless spares.

What the hell were they going to *do*?

Joy sat down a moment and played at unlacing her shoes while the boys both escaped up the stairs. Her father picked up the phone in the next room.

'Thomas Blake.' There was a pause and, when he spoke again, his voice had shifted from anxious to annoyed. 'Dad? What are you doing calling at this time of night? Don't tell me you forgot about the time difference.'

Tension clenched a fist round Joy's heart, and she lost her grip on the laces. Grandpa Blake couldn't *know*, could he?

The thought of him ever discovering how they'd betrayed his trust made her stomach hurt. She knew she ought to grab the phone off her dad and confess everything, but she simply didn't have the guts to do it.

'What? Why?' Her father's temper was obviously rising, for the words were growing steadily more clipped. 'What reason could you possibly have for—?

No! Forget it. Get somebody else to do it if you're that worried about it. I'm not getting involved. *Goodnight*, Dad.' He thumped the phone down with a grunt of frustration.

Joy didn't dare stick around to find out what Grandpa had wanted. She headed upstairs, to find her brother and Eilersen arguing already.

'Look, Blake, if you're such an expert, then how did it all go wrong in the first place?'

'I didn't *say* I was an expert, I said I know more about it than you! But you can't bear that, can you? As soon as anybody gets ahead of you in anything—'

'Grandpa just phoned,' Joy interrupted worriedly.

Justin bolted upright from where he was lying back on the bed. 'Did you speak to him?'

'I couldn't! Dad got it.' She bit her lip in dismay.

'Where is your grandfather? Can you call him back?' Eilersen asked urgently.

'No!' Joy jiggled on the spot as she struggled to get across the impossible situation. 'He's in America, he doesn't have a mobile and he didn't leave a contact number—'

'Do one four seven one,' said Justin.

Eilersen rolled his eyes. 'It doesn't work with international numbers.' He turned on Joy incredulously. 'Why the *hell* didn't you tell your dad you needed to speak to him?'

'You don't get it!' she blurted. 'Dad just won't listen to anything about the occult. The second he hears me say something about magic to Grandpa he's just going to yank the phone out of the wall or something! There's no way I'd have got a chance to say anything.'

Dad would never believe Dracherion was real. But he *would* believe they'd been brainwashed and try to cut them off from anything of Grandpa's that might actually help them.

There were footsteps on the stairs, and Joy slipped away down the landing to her own room as her mother showed up with a sleeping bag for Eilersen.

Joy had only meant to fake going to sleep to satisfy her parents, but the next thing she knew, she was snapping awake in her darkened room, with the clock on the VCR flashing three twenty. She was still dressed, and for a moment she stared at the ceiling in confusion, unable to even remember getting up to turn the light off.

Something had woken her. She didn't know what, but she could still sense it, that tiny flicker of something off that said the air currents had changed or the temperature was wrong or some other barely perceptible thing had shifted.

Joy slipped out of bed as silently as she could and stood in the middle of the room for so long, she was beginning to believe it had been her imagination. And then, as stealthy as a whisper, she heard it.

The creak of someone moving on the landing.

hoever was out there was trying very hard not be heard. Trying even harder than you'd expect at three o'clock in the morning. Joy's fists clenched, searching for a weapon, but there was nothing in the bedroom that could help her.

She moved to the door and carefully closed her hand around the doorknob. There was an art to twisting it very, very slowly, one hand pressing the door back against its frame so the click was as muffled as possible . . .

It wasn't quite muffled enough. The noise seemed gunshot-loud in the darkness. Her night-sight was defective, ruined by the bright streetlights close to her window, and she couldn't see the shadow that shouldn't be there until it moved.

'Quiet!' The disapproving tone of the whisper identified it as Eilersen.

Eilersen, wandering around her house in the small hours of the morning. Joy hugged her arms against her chest. She could scarcely make him out, certainly couldn't see his eyes, and she couldn't help but wonder if they might be solid black.

'Justin's gone.'

'What?' That startled her, an attack from an unexpected direction. She moved to the next doorway and saw from the glint of light on rumpled covers that it was true. 'Where did he go?'

'I woke and he was gone.' Eilersen's terse voice told her nothing. She couldn't read him well enough to guess what he was thinking.

Had Justin left of his own volition, or been taken? And what was Eilersen doing lurking in the hallway? She had no way of knowing if he'd been on his way to wake her, or trying to sneak past without her noticing. Had he done something to her brother?

Or was it Justin who was up to no good, creeping away in the middle of the night?

Dracherion could be in control of any one of them. How was she supposed to know who she could trust?

There was a soft creak, and a floorboard shifted beneath her feet as Eilersen moved towards the stairs. Joy found herself frantically trying to dredge up memories from before: had he always moved so carefully, been so sure-footed? He was in her brother's year at school – she barely knew him. How was she supposed to tell if this was still Eilersen, or something else entirely?

She didn't know, but she had no choice but to follow him down the stairs. As they rounded the curve of the spiral staircase, the dark got darker, no longer even a dribble of light from under the curtains to aid her. And it was cold – bitterly, bitingly cold, like the worst kind of Arctic wind had found its way indoors.

Eilersen halted abruptly, and she bit back a gasp as she walked into his elbow. He was gripping the banister tightly; she couldn't tell what had stopped him until she realized just why it was freezing.

The front door was standing open.

After a moment's hesitation they both approached the door. There were footprints in the snow outside, but Joy couldn't tell from the scuffed and overlaid prints whether someone had come in or gone out. The sky was calm; no more snow was falling, so she couldn't know how long they'd been there.

Eilersen paused in the hallway, perhaps listening, and then cautiously stepped through the open door. There was enough light from the streetlights to outline him at last, and she realized with a stab of wariness that he was fully dressed, right down to his coat and glasses.

How could she know that he hadn't made the prints himself and then come back upstairs to speak to her? She couldn't, but Justin was missing, and she didn't know what to do except slip her shoes on and follow him out.

Eilersen picked his way carefully down the path, his breath hanging in pale clouds in the frigid air. That reassured her somewhat: Joy was sure that a supernatural creature like Dracherion would have no need to mimic breathing. She wanted to be able to see his eyes, but in the half-light it was impossible to tell if they were any different from his natural dark brown.

He reached the gate but didn't open it, staring out into the quiet street beyond. 'Someone's walked along here. I can't tell if someone came in or went out.'

His voice was low, but it still seemed entirely too loud for a world where the only sounds were the wind and the soft crunch of snow underfoot. Joy glanced nervously over her shoulder and her heart leaped up into her throat.

'Daniel' – it suddenly seemed too impersonal to call him Eilersen – 'look at the door.'

He turned about swiftly, but his expression didn't flicker, and uncertainty still squeezed her like a vice.

The sight of the front door from this angle tore away all hope that this was a false alarm. Scratched into the glossy paintwork was a symbol; she didn't recognize it, but she knew instinctively that it had meaning, was more than just random graffiti. Like a stylized capital Y, with a zigzag on the down stroke, and little downward flicks at the sides that made her think of birds' wings.

Wings and a tail. Not quite a shape, but the suggestion of one; a symbol for a creature that had no real body of its own.

And if Dracherion had no body, then who had carved the shape into the door?

Something touched her shoulder, and Joy cringed away in horror. She was scarcely reassured when she realized it was Eilersen. His fingers were bony and icy cold, turning what might have been meant as a comforting touch into the death-grip of a corpse.

'That could have been done with Justin's knife,' he said softly.

'It could have been done with anything,' she countered apprehensively. If it *had* been scored into the door with her grandfather's bronze-handled knife, there were only two people who could have done it . . . and one of them had his hand on her shoulder right now.

The eye of her imagination painted the stab in the back so vividly that she wrenched away from him, but it was a sound inside the house that surprised them both. A soft, hollow, wooden noise of contact, like a door being gently pushed closed.

Eilersen glanced at her, then gestured with his head towards the house, somewhere between an order and an invitation.

He jostled her shoulder as they both tried to fit through the doorway, and she almost turned round and thumped him. She was as twitchy as a cornered cat and just about ready to attack the next thing that startled her.

The sound had come from somewhere in the direction of the kitchen. As Joy and Eilersen moved to flank the door leading to the dining room, she bent to pick up the carved wooden giraffe that served as a doorstop.

It was awkward to hold, but reassuringly weighty.

Quiet footsteps sounded in the room beyond; irregular, as if someone was moving uncertainly, or else taking pains to disguise their progress. Joy tensed and tightened her grip on the carving. A subtle shift in the position of the door warned her that someone had taken hold of the handle . . .

She was so focused on the door as it ponderously drew open that she didn't even see Eilersen's hand snake out to grip her wrist. Her downward strike went nowhere, and the wooden giraffe rebounded against the wall with a loud crack.

Justin stood blinking at them both from the doorway, hair in disarray and eyes filled with confusion. 'OK, what the hell are you guys doing?'

For a moment Joy could only stare at him. It was just as well Eilersen had stopped her. Whatever Justin had been doing, he didn't look much like an instrument of evil right now. In fact he looked barely awake, squinting hard to deal with even the dim light in the hallway.

Eilersen was not so easily reassured. 'Where did you go?' he asked intently.

'Oh, I'm sorry, should I have left a note?' Her brother's tone grew sharper as he woke up a little more. 'I went for a glass of water! Jesus, panic attack much?'

'You need shoes on to get a glass of water?' Eilersen said sceptically. He was alert, Joy had to give him that; she hadn't noticed her brother had his trainers on in addition to his pyjamas. She couldn't tell in the dark whether his shoes were wet from the snow.

Justin rolled his eyes. 'It was cold, OK! You don't need to be so jumpy.'

'Have you seen the front door?' Joy asked him nervously.

He frowned, seeming to realize for the first time that it was open. 'Did you guys go outside? It was closed when I came through a minute ago.'

'It was open when we came down.' Joy studied his face, but if he knew any more than he was letting on, it was very well disguised. The trouble was, she knew full well that Justin was an excellent liar.

'So . . . the door's mysteriously open?' he said, unimpressed.

'There's more,' said Eilersen flatly.

They led him outside to show him the symbol on the front door. He traced it with his fingers. 'So, what, this is some symbol of Dracherion's? Are we supposed to know what it means?'

'I don't think it's for our benefit,' Eilersen said. 'It's like the signs people used to put on the doors of houses where the occupants had the plague. A warning that those inside have been marked for death. As soon as it's taken over one of our bodies, the rest of us are doomed.'

'Well, that's cheerful,' Joy noted, hugging herself against the cold.

'Dad's going to *flip* when he sees this.' Justin poked at the carving. 'Look, it's not just scratched into the paintwork, it's been cut right into the wood.'

'What are we going to tell him?' Joy worried.

'Nothing.' Eilersen gave her a scornful look. 'About the most suspicious thing we could do right now is come up with a cover story. It'll just look like graffiti to your parents. They have no reason to connect it to us.'

'But don't they deserve some kind of warning?' Joy demanded. 'If you're right that Dracherion's marked the house, they could be in danger too.'

Eilersen sighed and rubbed his face, betraying a flash of uncertainty that broke the illusion of unnatural calm. 'They could . . . but if they are, there's nothing we can do about it. We have to hope that, for the moment, Dracherion's only going be interested in us . . . because if other people are in danger, there's no way to warn them. Who's going to believe us?'

'Grandpa Blake would,' Joy said heavily.

'And you're absolutely *sure* you can't contact him?' Eilersen said hopelessly.

'He didn't leave a phone number. He's travelling all round California; he probably won't even be in the same place by tomorrow. And he doesn't have a mobile or use email. Unless he calls us again, there's no way of getting hold of him before he's back on Monday.' She wished she'd been the one to pick up the phone tonight instead of Dad . . . but even if she had, would she have dared to confess what they'd done?

'We can't afford to wait that long,' Justin said. 'Dracherion knew my name and who I was. It must know Grandpa Blake's the biggest threat to it – and it probably knows exactly when he's due back. Whatever's going to happen, it's going to happen before Monday.'

They had two days, if that, to figure out a way to save their lives.

VII

Justin woke the next morning feeling like he had flu. His whole body ached and felt heavy, and the only thing that pierced through the fog was the pain in his hand.

The cut was shallower than he'd first feared, but it went right the way across his palm, from the base of his thumb to his little finger. He couldn't use his left hand at all without risking tearing it open. Even in his sleep he must have clenched his fists or something, for he'd woken in the night to find it bleeding.

Standing at the kitchen sink at three a.m., he'd found it easy to believe the bleeding would just keep going and never stop. He'd got light-headed, started thinking it was down to blood loss, and ended up having to sit on the floor until the dizzy spell passed. He supposed he might even have blacked out briefly. He hadn't heard the front door opening or any sound of the symbol being carved into it.

All in all, it wasn't exactly a moment he'd been keen to share with Eilersen. Besides, why should he be the only one who had to justify being out of bed? Eilersen hadn't given any reason for sneaking around himself. And what had possessed Joy to follow him about?

Justin shuddered at the unfortunate choice of words. Joy *could* have been possessed. Any one of them could. Someone had to have done the carving on the door.

Eilersen thought it was him, of course. Not that he had any actual *reason* – he just didn't like Justin. Well, Justin didn't see why he should need to explain himself to that idiot. *He* knew where he'd been last night, and he sure as hell hadn't been under the control of any spirit. If Dracherion had invaded his mind like that, he would know.

Surely he would know.

Where the hell *was* Eilersen, anyway? A cold finger of fear slid down Justin's spine as he took in the rolled-up sleeping bag. There was no telling how long the other boy had been gone.

He leaped out of bed and started pulling his clothes on, dialling Trevor on his mobile at the same time. He wanted all three of the others where he could see them. It wasn't safe for the four of them to be split up right now.

'J-Justin?' Judging by the tremble in his voice, Trevor was half expecting Dracherion to come flying out of the receiver.

Justin pulled his jumper over his head and trapped the phone between his ear and shoulder. 'Hey. Where are you?'

'At home?' Trevor said tentatively, as if worried it was the wrong answer.

'Yeah, well, get here,' Justin advised, crouching to look under the bed for his trainers. 'We've got to get this thing sorted – we can't afford to waste any more time.'

'Ah – Justin!' Trevor blurted quickly, before he

could move to hang up. 'Somebody— Something came to my house! There's a mark on the door—'

'Squiggly lightning-bolt thing? Yeah, we got one too. Eilersen reckons it's Dracherion's way of saying it knows where we live.' He decided to edit out the bit about being marked for death. 'But who knows, it might even help us. Maybe there'll be something about it in Grandpa Blake's books.'

'What if there's nothing there?' said Trevor pessimistically.

'Then we'll think of something else.' They still had the spellbook, after all, and he might well have found a solution already if Eilersen hadn't been hanging over his shoulder all night distracting him. 'Look, Trev, I've got to go. Just get over here.'

He hung up and sprinted downstairs.

He almost crashed into his father, who was just coming in the front door. 'Justin,' he said sharply, 'what do you know about this mark on the front door?'

'Mark? What kind of mark?' Hopefully his breathlessness disguised any sign of the lie as he followed his father outside. 'I didn't touch— Wow!'

Somehow, seen in daylight, the sigil was all the more disturbing. Just a few lines scored into the wood, but they served as a stark reminder that Dracherion had been here; that it could be here right now, while he was stuck making pointless conversation with his dad.

'Justin, if you know who did this—'

'I don't!' He knew he was sounding too defensive. His dad couldn't possibly think Justin really knew anything – he was just taking out his annoyance at the vandalism. 'I don't know anything about it, Dad, I swear,' he said more calmly. 'It wasn't like that last night.'

His father held his gaze for a long time and then sighed; probably not entirely convinced, but knowing he wouldn't get a better answer. 'All right. Your mother and I are going over to the retail park. We'll get some paint for the door while we're there. So if you *do* know who's responsible for this, they'd better not be coming back again.'

Justin decided it was best not to try and respond to that. 'Where's Joy?' he asked instead.

'Your sister's in the back garden with your friend.

Make sure you turn off the kitchen heater if both of you go out.'

'OK.' He all but sprinted away.

The back garden was blindingly coated with snow. Something about the appearance of the sky felt wrong; it seemed mismatched somehow, as if photos from two different days had been edited together. The day that this Saturday should have been, and the one the supernatural snow had made it.

Justin followed two sets of footprints round to the garage and listened at the side door for a few moments. There were faint sounds of somebody rummaging inside, but no voices. What was happening in there?

His mind immediately painted the image of Joy slumped in a pool of blood, while Eilersen hunted through the racks of tools for the best torture implements.

He swallowed hard and kicked the door open.

'What kept you?'

Joy barely even glanced his way, busy going through the drawers of their father's workbench. Eilersen stood rather stiffly to one side, probably not prepared to get his hands dirty.

Justin shot him a furious glare. 'Why didn't you wake me?' he demanded.

Eilersen gave him a look of contempt. 'You don't have an alarm set?'

'On a Saturday?'

'Oh, well, God forbid our imminent deaths should interfere with your lie-in,' he said snidely.

Justin transferred his attention to Joy before things could degenerate further. 'What are you doing in here?'

'Looking for my silver necklace.' She shoved one drawer closed and yanked open the next.

'Um . . . priorities?' he said incredulously.

'Um . . . yeah?' she echoed his tone obnoxiously. 'Grandpa gave it to me, remember? It might be important.'

'You really think it's here?' he grumbled, still annoyed. Why hadn't she come and got him for backup, instead of going off with Eilersen again? He didn't like the way they kept hanging around together.

'I don't know.' Joy shrugged, still searching. 'I never even used to go in here. And I lost it off the dining-room table, I'm sure, because I remember putting it

down there, and then when I came back, I couldn't—
Ah!'

She leaned so far forward that she practically
crawled into the drawer, and hooked something out
of the back of it. 'It *is* here,' she said, incredulous.
'How the hell did it get in Dad's workbench?'

Joy straightened up, disentangling the silver chain.
It was a handmade thing, the links all uneven sizes.
The pendant was a polished silver disc, engraved with
a complex pattern of lines within lines. A few days
ago Justin might have called it a snowflake or a
spider's web, but now . . .

'That looks a *lot* like last night's magic circle to
me,' said Eilersen.

'Grandpa Blake said it's supposed to block evil
influences,' Joy told him.

'Well, *yesterday* that might actually have been
useful.'

Justin opened his mouth for a retort, but swallowed
it unspoken. He could swear he'd just heard something – some sort of faint sound from the front of
the garage. He held up a hand for silence from the
others.

He listened. Nothing but the November wind and the faint thrum of traffic in the distance. Justin's shoulders gradually relaxed and he saw Eilersen scowl, about to speak—

And then it came again. A low, dull, wooden groan, like somebody pressing their weight against the bolted garage doors.

Justin exchanged a wary look with the others and began to pick his way towards the doors. It was difficult to move with any stealth when the front half of the garage was crammed with gardening equipment and old furniture.

Since their car had always stayed out on the driveway, the original wooden doors had never been replaced. The only thing holding them closed was a bolt at the top. Justin shot it aside in one violent motion and pushed the doors out, hard.

In the blinding spill of sunlight, all he could see for a moment was a dark, blurry shape, and he automatically jumped back. Then the silhouetted figure said, 'Ow,' and he realized it was Trevor.

'Jesus Christ, Trevor, knock!' he suggested, his heart rate slowly thumping its way back to normal.

'Sorry,' Trevor blurted, cringing. 'I was – um – I wasn't sure if it was you in there, so I was trying to see through the gap . . .'

'Yeah, yeah.' Justin patted him briefly on the shoulder. 'Come on, get in here. We were just looking for Joy's lost necklace.' He breathed out, trying to relax his jangled nerves.

'Did you find it?' Trevor asked, looking anxious.

'Yes, we did,' said Eilersen, behind him. He held the pendant gingerly by the chain and moved towards the light to examine it. 'The design is similar to the magic circle, so I assume it is supposed to be protective somehow. Whether it's anything that can help against Dracherion is another matter.'

'Let me see.' Justin reached to take it from Eilersen's hands, and Trevor jostled closer to him to get a better look.

As he seized hold of the silver disc, the cut across his palm became a white-hot line of pain. He let out a startled curse, and the pendant tumbled to the ground from his suddenly nerveless fingers.

VIII

'What happened?' Joy stared at Justin as he cradled his injured hand and blinked back tears of agony.

He was unable to speak for a moment, dizzied by pain. 'Nothing, I just . . . I forgot about my hand and I managed to grab hold of that in exactly the wrong place.'

The lie came automatically, while the rest of his brain was still trying to figure out exactly what *had* happened. The pendant had *burned* him – it wasn't just residual warmth, but scorching heat, like metal straight out of a fire. It hadn't touched anywhere near the cut, but the pain had been focused there, the way a bad earache could make itself felt in your teeth.

'Prat.' Joy rolled her eyes and stooped to rescue the necklace from the dusty floor. She showed no sign that the metal was even warm.

Justin flexed his hand gingerly, wondering what the flash of heat had meant. There was no way he'd imagined it – his eyes were still watering. Joy must have been right that there was magic in the necklace. But what had triggered it? Some trace of the ritual he'd performed still lingering in the cut?

Eilersen was watching him, a little too shrewdly for comfort. Had he also felt the heat? He'd only just begun to let go of the chain when Justin had taken the pendant.

Or was it *his* touch that had set it off, rather than Justin's?

Justin narrowed his eyes, but decided not to voice his suspicions for the moment. He cleared his throat awkwardly.

'Right. So, um . . . Grandpa Blake's house, then?' he said. 'There's got to be something there that can help us.'

If his parents came back and noticed the key gone, there would be trouble. But right now, his father being angry with him was absolutely the least of his problems.

The streets were surprisingly busy for such a cold day; the snow had brought people out. Most of it was gone from the roads by now, and on the pavement it had been stamped into slush. They walked briskly despite the slippery conditions, driven on by a shared sense of urgency.

'The same symbol was left on your door last night?' Eilersen asked Trevor.

He nodded in agitation. 'It was there when I woke up. I thought my mum was going to freak, but she just thought it was Gaz and his mates from up the road. They're always doing stuff like that to the houses down my way.'

'And you slept through the whole thing without hearing anything?' Eilersen prodded.

Trevor looked dismayed. 'I – um – I don't— My bedroom's right on the other side of the—'

'Oh, give it a rest, Eilersen,' Justin snapped. 'You

don't even know there was anything to hear. The only reason *you* woke up last night was because I got up to go for a glass of water. For all you know, that symbol just spontaneously *appeared* there and didn't make a sound.'

'Spontaneously appeared leaving footprints, apparently,' Eilersen said snottily.

'F-footprints?' Trevor's eyes went wide with alarm.

'Yes. I didn't have the chance to figure out exactly where they went – or came from' – this was said with a pointed look at Justin that made him scowl in response – 'but I'm still sure that whoever made that mark on the door was no spirit. Dracherion has no physical form of its own, remember? It has to have possessed a human body to do it. One of ours.'

Joy glanced at Trevor. 'Were there footprints outside your door too?'

He dipped his head sheepishly. 'I, er, I didn't – I didn't think to look.'

'Of course not. Why would you?' Eilersen said sarcastically, apparently to himself. Justin glared, but the other boy's long strides took him ahead, and he didn't glance back.

The chill in the air made the walk seem longer. By the time they reached his grandfather's street, Justin was more worn out than he'd have liked to admit, and Trevor was puffing and panting. He looked as bad as Justin felt, deep dark smudges under his eyes as if he'd been up all night.

Returning to the house made him feel like a burglar. Yesterday it had been easy to couch it as informal borrowing from family, but today they were planning to ransack the place. Eilersen marched straight on in, insensitive as ever, but Trevor seemed to shrink as he passed through the door.

Justin could definitely understand the feeling.

'We should probably search the whole house,' Joy suggested. She grimaced, obviously uncomfortable with the idea. 'Grandpa might have hidden something away from the rest of the collection, for security.'

'Obviously he didn't reckon on nefarious grand-children,' Eilersen muttered.

Justin ignored that, mostly because he couldn't think of a way to respond without digging himself in deeper. 'All right,' he agreed reluctantly. 'You two see what you can find in the study, and me and Joy will check out the rest of the house.' At least a study was kind of like an office, so he wouldn't feel quite so bad about Eilersen pawing around in there. 'We're looking for . . . Jesus, I don't know. Another spellbook, stuff about spirits – anything.' He shrugged helplessly.

'I'll take the living room and dining room,' Joy volunteered quickly, leaving him stuck with the bedroom. Great.

He *tried* not to peek into anything he shouldn't, but it was hard to sort papers without at least skim-reading. And some of it was dangerously tempting: in one folder he found what had to be his father's school reports, and the startling phrase 'can only make so many allowances for this behaviour' jumped out at him before he could look away.

A cardboard box under the bed, however, contained an even bigger puzzle.

The box was clearly very old – the elastic band around it had disintegrated into brittle fragments – but it looked as if at least some of the wear and tear had come from regular handling. Inside was a whole collection of photographs that Justin had never seen before.

Grandpa Blake was easy to recognize, even though he was about thirty years younger. It took longer to see the boy of seventeen or so as a younger version of his father; he had a much thinner face and surprisingly long hair, and a surly expression that made Justin want to snigger.

It was the first picture he'd ever seen of his father as a boy. He would have assumed, if he'd thought about it at all, that Grandpa simply hadn't owned a camera at that time, since there were plenty more recent family pictures on the mantelpiece. There were even some snaps of a few distant cousins, and an extremely old picture of his great-grandparents. Why were those on display, while his father's childhood pictures were hidden away?

There were two other people in the shot, one of them a woman who had to be his grandmother. Justin was surprised to see her; his father had said so little about her, beyond the fact that she'd died young, that he'd assumed it had happened when his dad was just a baby.

And then there was the little girl sitting on her knee. Who was she? Dad didn't have any siblings, nor even any girl cousins. Yet there she was, dressed up with her blonde hair in ringlets and clutching a rag doll, as if she belonged there. She looked about six years old.

This was getting weirder and weirder. Justin leafed through the rest of the photos. They were all from the same era or earlier: snapshots charted his father's growth from baby into teenager, but the pictures of the little girl stopped with the family portrait. He supposed there might be a box of later images somewhere, but it wasn't stored anywhere near the first.

There were some other photos too, of an even younger Lucien Blake, apparently from his university days. In one he could see a ring of candles in the background.

Justin sat up straighter, only now remembering the pressing reason for this search. He quickly emptied out the rest of the photographs and found a folded letter at the bottom of the box. It was handwritten and dated October, twenty-seven years ago.

Dear Lucien,
I am sorry to hear that Lilian's condition has worsened

again. I understand your desire to trust to the supposed experts in this matter, but the fact is that their science is failing you. Why wait for a miracle to descend from the sky when the means to work our own is within our grasp?

I know that Mary disapproves of our endeavours, but I have faith in your ability to persuade her to assist us, for Lilian's sake. We will have to discuss the question of our fourth when I arrive. Expect me at noon or there-abouts this Saturday, and let us be optimistic that this sad occasion for a reunion will soon become a happy one.

Yours in friendship,
Anthony

Justin carefully refolded the letter, as much confused as enlightened by its contents. He had no idea who this Anthony was, but Grandpa Blake had obviously contacted him about some enchantment to help Lilian – whoever *she* was. But what the letter implied about Grandpa's reluctance and desperation was disturbing . . . and the reference to finding a fourth struck a troubling chord.

Of course, it had to be a coincidence. No doubt hundreds of different rituals required four people. And even if his grandfather *had* once summoned spirits, there was absolutely no reason to believe that he had encountered Dracherion.

No reason, except for the fact that Dracherion had mentioned him . . .

A shadow fell over him, and Justin flinched in alarm, cracking his head on the edge of the bed. His sister threw her hands up in apology. 'Whoa, whoa! Jumpy.'

He rubbed his head and scowled up at her. 'Ow. OK, with the evil killer spirit chasing us around, a *little* warning might be good.'

'I *did* knock,' she said petulantly. 'So did you find anything?'

'Not really.' He shuffled everything back into the box and shoved it under the bed. 'Grandma Blake's name was Mary, wasn't it?'

'Mary Penelope,' she agreed promptly. 'I looked it up on Dad's birth certificate when I had to do that family tree thing for school. There's no point asking him anything – I had to leave half that side of the tree blank. I bet he'd have cut Grandpa off too, if he'd had the chance. Why?'

'Just wondered.' Justin pushed himself up with a groan, legs protesting. 'So you wouldn't know if we have any relatives called Lilian on that side?'

Joy shrugged. 'Not so far as I know. Is it important?'

'Probably not.' He sighed. 'Come on, this is a bust. I already knew there wouldn't be anything outside of the main collection.'

He didn't really believe there'd be anything there, either. He'd never seen anything else like the book in all the time he'd spent looking. It was one of a kind.

As they re-entered the study, he saw Trevor sitting in the corner glumly leafing through a book, and Eilersen cross-legged on the floor with a towering pile beside him. 'What have you found?' he asked them.

'Not enough,' said Eilersen. 'At least your grandfather is more organized than you. He's got a decent indexing system – but that doesn't help when the information isn't there. The stuff in these books is . . . scrappy, at best, and a lot of it's contradictory.'

He frowned at the pile, as if they'd been written that way deliberately, just to spite him.

'So what *do* we know?' Joy asked, sitting down opposite him.

'A little bit more about spirits.' Eilersen pulled his glasses off and rubbed the bridge of his nose. 'From what I've read, the realm they come from is . . . not nice. They'd rather live in our world, but they can't get here themselves – it takes energy to be here, the way it takes fuel for a plane to stay up in the sky. They resent us because we get to live here, and they hate it even more when people use magic to push them around. They'll take any chance they can to attack a human. The only way to be truly safe is if you know the spirit's real name.'

'Which we don't,' Justin put in grimly.

'If you call it by name, the spirit is forced to obey you. Without that, it's just going to turn on you the first opportunity it gets. Weaker spirits merely go in for spiteful mischief . . . the really nasty ones kill and maim and cause disasters.' He grimaced. 'Somehow, I don't think Dracherion is a weaker spirit.'

'But can't we just wait it out?' Trevor asked tentatively. 'If it has to run out of energy sooner or later . . .'

Eilersen shook his head. 'No. That's the thing – it doesn't. Because we, in our ultimate wisdom' – he shot a pointed look at Justin – 'hooked it up with a constant supply. By giving Dracherion some of our blood and hair, some of our substance, we allowed it to draw the power it needed to stay here from *us*. The idea being that the formal banishment at the end of the ritual would cut that connection off.'

'Except we didn't *finish* the banishment,' Joy said, looking sick.

'So we'll do it now,' Justin said, grabbing hold of the book of magic.

'You can't,' Eilersen told him, all but rolling his eyes. 'The banishment that's in that book is to release the spirit safely from the circle. It isn't *in* the circle any more. You might as well try to pour a bottle of milk down the sink once it's already smashed on the floor.' He put his glasses back on. 'And that isn't all.'

'Of course it isn't.' Justin leaned back with a groan.

'Spirits try to possess people because it's like a free pass to stay in this world. Our bodies *belong* here – if Dracherion can steal one of them, it won't need to keep burning energy to stay. And the only reason it hasn't killed us yet is because we're supplying that energy.' He eyed the other three.

'Dracherion must have used one of our bodies to carve those symbols on the doors. It doesn't have a physical presence of its own – it has powers it can use, but it can't *touch* anything. Not unless it possesses someone.'

'Well, it wasn't me, so you can stop giving me that look.' Justin glowered at him.

'You don't know that,' Eilersen countered. 'The person who was possessed might not even remember it afterwards. It could be any one of us.' He swept a meaningful look over the others. 'Whoever it was, you can bet Dracherion will come after them again. I'm guessing it can't keep the possession up for long, or else the rest of us would be dead already. But once it's got strong enough to crush the human personality completely, it'll settle into that body and never have to leave. And once *that* happens . . .'

He didn't finish the sentence. He didn't need to.

'**S**o what now?' Joy asked, clearly agitated. They'd kept on fruitlessly searching at Grandpa Blake's until hunger forced them out. Now they were walking down the street eating burgers. None of them could bear the thought of sitting down to eat while precious seconds ticked away.

'It's obvious we're not going to find anything else to help,' Justin insisted. 'We've got to go back to the book. If we can find some other ritual—'

'You're crazy!' his sister protested. 'After the way the last one went?'

'Well, we can't just sit around and wait for it to

get us!' The others' refusal to act was driving Justin nuts. It was obvious to him that the book was the only weapon they had, but they were all too scared of another ritual going wrong to even think about it.

But if they didn't use more magic, then what options did they have? You couldn't pick a fight with something that didn't even have a body.

'Maybe we should try to make a deal with Dracherion,' Trevor suggested timidly. 'If we offered to help it . . . give it more power or something . . .'

Justin snorted in disbelief. 'What are we going to do, sacrifice chickens? You want to spend the rest of your life as a slave to this thing?'

For a moment he actually thought that Trevor might flare up with anger, but then he just looked at the floor. 'It's *too powerful*, Justin!' he said plaintively. 'What are we supposed to do?'

'Something!' Justin retorted. 'Anything. Not just give up without a fight.' He considered. 'We'll go back to the park. Have a look around. There might be something there that we missed last night.'

The others didn't seem convinced, but they followed him anyway. A grim mood had settled over the group once it became clear that no easy answer was forthcoming. Not that Justin had really expected one. He'd realized from the beginning that they'd have to take risks; the trouble was, the others wouldn't listen to him.

Trevor wasn't a problem – terrified or not, he'd go along with any plan Justin came up with – but Eilersen would argue if he said the sky was blue. And as for Joy . . .

Joy was hanging around with Eilersen too much. Whether Dracherion was steering her or she was just falling for his know-it-all persona, it was bad news. If he couldn't trust even his sister to back him up, he might have to take things into his own hands. They couldn't afford to waste time arguing over everything.

The park was almost empty when they reached it, the only signs of life a couple huddled on a bench and an old man walking his dog. The slumped remains of a half-hearted snowman stood by the park gates, but otherwise only a slushy mess remained of the supernatural snowfall. Justin hadn't bothered to specify how long the snow should last, so Dracherion must have let it come to a natural end rather than waste much-needed energy keeping it going.

Their bikes were still chained to the front fence where they'd left them. Justin strode past without a second glance, but his sister called him back. 'Justin! Look at this.'

Somebody had slashed the tyres on both bikes – not just slashed, in fact, but thoroughly hacked up, the damage far beyond the little needed to make the bikes unusable. Justin swore creatively.

'What's wrong?' Trevor stumbled over to join them. 'Oh.' He paled at the sight of the bikes. 'Do you – do you think Dracherion might have done that?'

Justin shook his head. No need to get completely paranoid; this was surely way too petty for an evil spirit bent on revenge. 'Slashing tyres? Why would it bother? Nah, it's just some kid who thinks it's funny.' He kicked the fence in exasperation. 'Guess we'll be leaving the bikes here for the moment.'

They caught up with Eilersen over at the tennis courts. 'Somebody's been here before us,' he said as he rose from his crouch.

'Yeah, like, three quarters of the kids in town.' Justin frowned. 'What d'you mean?'

'I mean that the candles we left behind have disappeared, and the snow's been cleared away from around the circle – *only* around the circle, as if whoever did it already knew it was there to find. And take a look at this.' He indicated the shapes he'd drawn the previous night. Justin saw that the circle was no longer simply chalked onto the surface, but somehow burned in, as if some super-heated metal device had been left there long enough to melt the tarmac.

'I'm surprised Dracherion didn't destroy all traces of the ritual,' Joy said. 'Just to prove that it really is free.'

'Maybe it can't,' said Eilersen. He ran a finger thoughtfully over the rim of the circle. 'After all, it's not as if the circle was made incorrectly – Dracherion just used the snow to erase part of it. What's left here may still have some power.'

'Perhaps, but that alone won't be enough to save you.' A voice spoke up from behind them.

A very *familiar* voice. They all whirled round.

'Grandpa?' Joy blurted in disbelief.

Justin half thought he was hallucinating, but no, it really was their grandfather. He was dressed for sunnier weather, in a white polo shirt and the floppy-brimmed hat he wore for gardening, but the grim set of his jaw and his folded arms belied the relaxed image.

Justin swallowed. 'Er . . . hi, Grandpa, you're . . . back early . . .'

He let his bag slowly slump to the ground behind him, as if his grandfather would somehow know at a glance that the book was inside it. He'd returned the knife before they'd left the house and had been glad to be rid of it, but he hadn't been prepared to let the book out of his sight.

'Yes. I am.' Grandpa Blake's voice was curt, and with the sun directly behind him and the hat shading his eyes, it was hard to make out much of his expression.

Justin's insides turned to ice-water. All of a sudden he couldn't help but think that Grandpa's first reaction to what they'd done was probably *not* going to be to pat them on the head and reassure them that he'd take care of everything.

'Um . . . so why'd you come home?' he asked nervously.

His grandfather scowled. 'You know very well why I'm here. Did you really think, after all you've seen, that I would have no way of detecting what goes on in my own house?'

Justin's heart sank. 'So you knew right from the beginning.'

'Do you have *any* idea what you've done?' Grandpa Blake demanded. 'And you, Joy – why didn't you stop this? You like to imagine you're so much more mature than your brother, but the truth is you're the first to follow wherever he drags you.'

Joy flinched as if she'd been kicked in the stomach, and Justin was feeling more than a little nauseated himself. He hadn't thought Grandpa Blake would be exactly thrilled at their actions, but he hadn't expected this kind of vitriol either.

He looked at the ground. 'Grandpa, we didn't—'

'You didn't what? Didn't *mean* to break into my house? *Accidentally* stole from me? Summoned a being far beyond your understanding purely by mistake?' Grandpa Blake's voice was absolutely thunderous.

111

'We didn't know it was *real*!' Justin blurted. 'OK, it was stupid, it was a bad thing to do, but how were we supposed to know it was *dangerous*? You never told us – Dad always said we shouldn't believe any of it . . .'

'Ah, yes, your *father*.' The level of venom packed into that one word was frightening. 'Dear Thomas, always *so* convinced that the nasty truths would go away if you ignored them. He's done you no favours by burying your heads in the sand beside his own.' Grandpa Blake heaved an angry sigh. 'Still, I suppose the blame is partly mine. I should never have let that book out of my sight for a moment. Although I could be forgiven for not imagining *my own grandchildren* would be the ones to steal it.'

Justin winced.

'But perhaps things can be rescued,' Grandpa Blake continued briskly. 'Where is the book? If we cast the right enchantments straight away, there may still be a chance to undo the terrible damage you've done.'

He really only hesitated for a second, but before he could even make a move, Trevor was ahead of him. 'It's here,' he blurted breathlessly, sweeping up the bag from the ground. 'The book's in here.'

Justin sighed and plucked the bag out of his friend's grip. Did Trevor have to make it look like he wouldn't have volunteered? 'I didn't think it was safe to leave it at—'

'Enough,' his grandfather cut him off curtly. 'I'm not interested in hearing your justifications. Bring it here.'

When his grandfather used that voice, disobeying was not an option. Justin had crossed half the distance between them before—

'Wait!' The shout caught him off guard, and he automatically stopped to glance back. Eilersen grabbed him by the arm to hold him still.

'What are you *doing*?' Trevor gasped in dismay.

'Being cautious,' he said shortly. He fixed an intent look on the face beneath the floppy hat. 'You're Lucien Blake?'

'The word of my grandchildren isn't good enough for you?' Grandpa Blake spoke with a curled lip and affected amusement, but Justin could tell by the set of his shoulders that he was annoyed.

'Under the circumstances . . . not really.' Eilersen was pale and tense, the tiny hints of his controlled uneasiness somehow twice as contagious as obvious panic. When he stepped back, Justin stepped with him.

His grandfather chuckled, but there wasn't any humour in the sound. 'You learned the value of caution a little too late, I think . . . but very well – ask your questions. I can answer anything you like, but time is short, and getting shorter.'

'I'm sure you could,' Eilersen said tightly. 'But I don't think that proves anything. Take off your hat, please.'

Grandpa Blake's face grew taut, as if he suspected he was being made fun of. 'I'm not about to play games.'

'I'd just like to see your eyes,' Eilersen continued implacably.

Justin swallowed as he realized that the pattern of shadows prevented him from seeing whether his grandfather's eyes were their normal bright blue . . . or something else entirely.

He took another step backwards.

'We have *no time* for this,' his grandfather empha-sized. 'Dracherion is trying to divide us and distract us even now.'

'Just give it to him, Justin,' Trevor pleaded, clearly petrified of angering the old man even further.

'*Don't* do it,' Eilersen ordered.

Justin didn't know which way to turn. If his grand-father was right, every second they were delayed could be deadly. If Eilersen was right . . .

He shot an anguished glance at his sister – in time to see her carefully unwinding the silver chain from around her neck. He took another step backwards, away from both Eilersen and his grandfather, and gave her a subtle nod.

'Grandpa . . . catch!' she said slowly.

The necklace was an awkward missile, but the throw was strong and true, and the pendant spun through the air straight towards him.

Or it would have done, if he'd still been there.

As the necklace reached the point where it should have hit home, Joy saw the image of her grandfather stream away like butter under a blowtorch. A derisive chuckle filled the air as the glowing blue-black figure of the boy sprang up in its place.

Joy glanced around nervously to see if there were witnesses, but the park was now completely deserted. Had Dracherion waited until they were alone to make its move, or had it driven the park's other occupants away?

Just how powerful was it already?

'Now, now, children, does my guise not please you?' the spirit chided. 'Then how about this one? Or this?' It passed through a succession of steadily more gruesome transformations.

'We weren't fooled,' Justin said boldly. He swallowed hard but stood his ground as the spirit once more became his duplicate, prowling towards him.

'Oh, of course not.' Dracherion smirked, flashing teeth too sharp to belong in any human mouth. '*How were we supposed to know it was dangerous?*' it quavered in a cruel imitation. It made a patting gesture towards his cheek like an affectionate elderly aunt, and he flinched. 'Poor little defenceless Justin, how were you *ever* to know? Who would have thought that rituals of blood and death and darkness could possibly be harmful?'

Joy steeled herself and sprinted forward to snatch up the necklace from the grass. She held it out in front of her, feeling absurdly like a police officer flashing her badge. 'We know what you are, and we have defences now,' she said shakily. 'You can't touch us.'

'You truly believe such a trinket can defeat me?'

The spirit laughed delightedly. 'How . . . positively charming.' Dracherion shrank into the shape of Joy as a little girl, complete with gappy teeth and the wholly embarrassing glittery pink jumper she'd once thought was the greatest thing ever.

'If we're no threat to you, why would you need to trick us into giving up the book?' Eilersen said. 'You don't have a body. You can't touch it. So what good does it do you? The only reason to try to get it out of our hands is because you don't want *us* to have it.'

Dracherion's black eyes, incongruous in the middle of a small round freckled face, narrowed. 'Make no mistake, *boy*,' the girl spat, 'I can destroy you whenever it suits me. My vessel is already chosen, and the possession cannot be stopped. The artefacts you hold are worthless against my true power, even in the hands of far wiser mortals than you.'

'Yeah, but you're not at full power *yet*, are you?' Justin said defiantly.

Despite her brother's boldness, Joy couldn't quite quell a shudder. What if it was true? *My vessel is already chosen* . . . She eyed the others around her uneasily. Which one of them could it be? What if it was *her*?

'You know nothing of true strength and weakness, human child,' the spirit said, fury blending into a more disturbing dark amusement. 'You live your lives on a scale beneath notice. Do the ants you step on care if you are at full strength? But the ants are more your kindred than you will ever be mine. You are animals and puppets, crude creatures of flesh like the beasts that crawl around you. Perhaps it is time you learned your place among them.'

The figure splintered apart with the force of an explosion, the blue-black flames real enough that heat licked over Joy as she ducked. Trevor cried out, and Justin hit the ground, hugging the book protectively to his chest as they stared around for Dracherion's next appearance.

It didn't come. Instead, as Justin stood up and Joy slowly lowered her arms, they could hear a strange buzz, like the noise in the school assembly hall before the teachers called for quiet. The overlapping sounds weren't voices, though, but something else. A rapid, ceaseless beating, like hundreds of skin drums being struck, and beyond that a cacophony of chattering, shrieking, cackling, screeching . . .

Joy looked up, and the sky was alive. Dark clouds were boiling across it like smoke from a blaze, but it wasn't ash or dust carried on the wind that she was seeing. This was something living, something *flocking*, a multitude of winged forms bearing down towards them, blotting out the sky.

'Bats?' yelped Justin incredulously, shielding his eyes.

'Birds,' said Eilersen, and it should have seemed ridiculous, harmless, but not *this* many birds, zeroing in on their position with such speed and sense of purpose. They were spilling out of the trees and over the rooftops: sparrows and crows and gulls and doves and more that Joy didn't recognize, gathering together in one unnatural monster swarm.

For it was a swarm, not any ordinary flock. They didn't *move* like birds; instead they crowded the skies like some biblical plague of insects, ready to cut a swathe through the landscape and turn green fields to desert. In her mind's eye, Joy could already see beaks and talons tearing, beady eyes glaring from all directions, brutally battering wings.

She started to run.

The others needed no prompting to run with her, tearing across the park and through the playground with the speed of desperation. The slushy snow was lethal, their feet sinking where the thaw had touched and sliding where it hadn't.

Longer legs made all the difference; even Eilersen's awkward loping stride and Trevor's headlong stumble were outpacing Joy. Her beaten-up old trainers were worn too smooth to grip, and her breath was already burning in her chest. Her ankle caught and twisted, and she staggered.

'Keep moving!' Eilersen snapped at her, as if she needed to be told.

'Come on, Joy!' pleaded Trevor with a panicked look over his shoulder. She made the mistake of glancing up at the sky.

The birds were following in their wake like a ribbon of smoke chasing after a steam train. The noise was incredible – she would never have believed that birds alone could be so loud.

'Where?' she blurted out as they reached the park gates, knowing their chances of escaping on foot were next to nothing. She flinched as a flight of chattering magpies burst out of the trees ahead, passing so close that the beat of their wings whipped at her hair.

'Downhill,' gasped her brother, unable to spare any extra words of explanation. Joy doubted he had anything so grand as a plan, just the desperate hope of evading pursuit for a few moments more.

'We need to get indoors!' Trevor cried, shielding his head with his hands as a vicious-looking crow swooped entirely too low for comfort. Birds were landing on the park fence and immediately launching themselves again, compelled to keep chasing by a power that overrode their natural instincts.

'There isn't anywhere!' Joy objected. It was all residential streets on the route into town; hills and hedgerows if they went the other way. No public buildings for miles, and their own home was too far away.

'Under the trees, then,' Justin said. 'If we can get onto Potts Hill, we can head for that nature trail bit . . .'

Joy half turned to glance at him, but then something tangled itself in her hair. She swore and batted at it madly.

There were birds everywhere, flying blind and

crashing into them every way they turned. Each impact was jarringly hard; they could hear the gruesome crunch of lightweight bones and see dead or injured birds dropping around them. It was all the more horrifying to realize that this was no concerted attack, but a multitude of living creatures being pelted at them as if they were no more than missiles. Dracherion wasn't commanding these birds, just crudely taking charge of their movements, like a kid with a remote-control toy.

'How much further?' called Eilersen from somewhere off behind her.

'Does it matter?' Justin grunted. It wasn't as if they had any choice but to keep moving. The air was thick with flying bodies and falling feathers, wings battering their faces and beaks scratching their skin.

'Oof!' Joy lost her balance as someone smacked into her from behind, knocking what little wind she still had out of her lungs.

'Sorry, sorry!' Trevor gabbled anxiously. He clutched at her shoulder to right them both, snagging the chain of her necklace in the process and almost tearing it clean off.

'Watch it!' She clapped a hand over the pendant to protect it and found the metal fiery hot. A whole lot of use the warning was right now. And even if there was some magic to it that stopped Dracherion attacking her directly, it wasn't doing a thing against this aerial bombardment.

A jackdaw landed on the path right in front of her, and Joy almost tripped over her own feet dancing around it. She smacked the back of her hand against a tree trunk as she twisted. There was a burst of hot, nauseating pain and she squeezed her eyes shut and spat swearwords.

'Joy? You all right?' Her brother heard her cry out and hung back to rejoin her as she cradled her wrist.

'*Ow,*' was all she could find the presence of mind to say.

Justin slung an awkward arm over her shoulder to help drag her onwards.

They were at the top of Potts Hill now, and the going was even harder. The downhill path was pitted and uneven, buried under drifts of leaves and lingering snow. The tall hedgerows were no protection as birds rocketed in and out, causing the springy branches to whip back and scratch at them.

'We're almost there – come on, just don't slow down!' Justin insisted.

But Joy found it hard to force herself to keep moving. She wondered if this was what it felt like to be stoned to death; impact after impact, until it didn't matter that they were small because you just knew they were never going to stop. And the fact that the projectiles were alive only made it worse; knowing that every collision hurt the birds even more than it hurt her, feeling the panicked creatures nip and scratch and scrabble, kicking and stepping on their fragile bodies because there was just nowhere else to put her feet . . .

'Joy, come on!' In a daze of pain and misery, she barely realized that she'd reached their destination.

She was distantly aware of scrambling over the wooden gate, Eilersen's bony hand on her good arm helping to pull her over. Justin was saying something to her, but the words weren't penetrating, and she couldn't seem to concentrate. He looked worried.

He also looked rather fuzzy around the edges, and Joy had a nasty suspicion she was on the verge of passing out. She managed to stagger a few steps more down the beaten track, then ran out of strength and willpower, and sat down hard in the dirty snow.

'Joy!' Her brother pulled at her – God, couldn't he leave her *alone* . . . ?

'Wait!' Eilersen blessedly stopped him in mid-shake. 'Something's happening.'

Joy looked up and saw the birds coming to roost in the trees all around them. The branches were winter bare, small protection from the bombardment, but for some reason it was stopping anyway.

'What are they *waiting* for?' her brother muttered, sounding almost indignant.

'Just to freak us out even more,' Joy muttered darkly to herself. Dracherion wasn't just trying to *get* them – it was trying to make them suffer. Birds might not be enough to kill them, but the more the spirit harassed them, the less strength they would have left to fight off its attempts at possession. A tired, frightened mind and weakened body had to be easier to take control of than one that was strong and healthy.

Justin folded his arms and tried to recapture some bravado. 'Yeah? Well, it takes more than a bunch of flying feather dusters to intimidate me. Stop staring!' he yelled upwards, waving his arms aggressively. Any ordinary bunch of birds would have taken flight . . . but these were a long way from ordinary.

For a moment everything was still and silent, but for the sounds of shifting feathers and ragged breathing.

And then the rustling started.

XI

The sound came from everywhere at once, the irregular susurration of things moving through the underbrush; small, fast, numerous things, hundreds of them, thousands of them, surging over tree roots and through drifts of fallen leaves . . .

'Rats!' Trevor yelled, jumping to his feet.

There were rats.

They stampeded out of the trees like startled cattle in a Western, an undulating wave of grey-brown bodies. Joy barely had time to jump to her feet before there were rodents all over her.

There were so many rats they created a traffic jam, those further back scrambling over the leaders. They scrabbled their way up her trouser legs, paws catching and teeth tearing at the material. One had crawled up under her coat and almost made it into her shirt, and she shook it off and flung it away with a cry of revulsion.

Justin was in even worse straits – his body was absolutely *crawling* with rats, as if he was sending out some signal to attract them. 'How do I get them *off*?' he demanded desperately, hopping and shaking his arms as one tried to wriggle up his sleeve. There were just too many of the things to brush away; every one that fell to the ground was replaced by half a dozen more.

'Justin, your bag!' Eilersen warned. There were rats trying to crawl inside it. Justin shook one out, and held the bag up high above his head. Joy's heart lurched at the thought of how quickly the creatures could shred the spellbook if they got in there.

'Toss it over here, Justin!' Trevor called. He was almost in the clear, off to one side where the rats flowed round instead of over him. She saw her brother contemplate the throw, but he clearly didn't dare to try it. If he fumbled it and the bag plopped down into that seething carpet . . .

Joy squawked and jumped as a rat dropped onto her shoulders from above. They were up in the trees now; the birds in the upper branches were shifting restlessly, caught between their instinct to flee the rodent tide and the compulsion to stay.

'Your necklace!' Eilersen shouted across to her, as another rat scrabbled at her coat sleeve.

'I know!' They were obviously after it, but she didn't know how to protect it.

'No, give me your necklace!'

'What?' Joy was confused, but she had to trust he had a plan. She didn't even try to lift the chain over her head, just yanked until it came free, hoping the links would bend rather than fracture.

'Here!' Eilersen cupped his hands, but he wasn't close enough for her to hand it to him. She grimaced and leaned out, trying to judge the throw. A group of magpies came shooting down from the upper branches, and she yanked back her hand hastily.

'I can't throw it!' she called to him, shaking her

head. It would just be snapped up out of the air if she tried. The pendant cut into her hand as she clenched her fingers around it, determined not to lose her grip and drop it.

'I know! Just stay there.' Eilersen was trying to wade through the sea of rats towards her, shielding his head with his arms now the birds had got back in the act. They were dive-bombing Justin, and he had to drop the bag back down and hug it against his chest.

'Whatever you're doing, do it faster!' he yelped.

'I'm *aware* of the urgency, thank you,' Eilersen snapped back.

'It's all right for you, you're not the one with *rats* trying to crawl up your— Jesus!' Justin was shaking his whole body like a dog fresh out of a muddy puddle, trying vainly to dislodge the writhing creatures.

'Toss it to me, Justin!' Trevor called again, but Justin couldn't even straighten up, never mind take proper aim.

'Here, quickly.' Eilersen had finally succeeded in getting within arm's length, and prised the necklace out of Joy's tight fist. As soon as he pulled away from her, the focus of the attack shifted to him; rats poured off her and the tree behind her, skittering down her body and leaping from her shoulders.

Rats from a sinking ship, she thought dazedly as she slumped back against the tree. Her injured wrist was throbbing like crazy, and her chest ached as if somewhere in the chaos she'd forgotten to keep breathing.

Justin was almost doubled over now in his bid to curl up defensively. 'Eilersen, if you've *got* a plan—' he grated.

'*Working* on it,' Eilersen grunted back, and then sank down on one knee, groping for something amidst the heaving mass of rats.

'What are you doing?' Trevor cried out in dismay. 'Don't – Joy, don't let him lose it!'

Joy couldn't do anything; Eilersen was already too far away from her. She could only stare helplessly into the cluster of rats where he knelt, praying for a glimpse of silver that didn't come. Had he dropped the necklace? If he had, they were doomed – the rats would surely bear it away in moments.

But wait – it didn't look like he was searching. It was hard to see what he was doing, but he wasn't groping along the ground; more like fighting to drag his hand through the mob of rats running over it. What was he trying to do?

Justin let out a pained cry, and Joy spun back towards him in time to see him hit the ground and curl up like a hedgehog. He was so densely buried in rats that she wasn't sure he could breathe, and yet still the birds swooped down on him. How could they even find a sliver of flesh to peck?

'*Daniel!*' she yelled frantically as she tried to fight her way through to her brother. Rats squirmed and wriggled under her feet, and she was sick with horror at the thought of tripping and falling among them.

'Almost . . . Got it!' Eilersen finished, straightening up triumphantly. He'd come round in a big loop to the place where he'd begun, but Joy couldn't see what he thought he'd achieved. The rats were still swarming, the birds were still diving . . .

Or were they?

The clearing was still full of flapping birds, but they no longer seemed to have a sense of purpose. They would come swooping down out of the trees, then veer away at the last minute, as if suddenly confused. The rats were milling, still running over her feet and Justin's body, but no longer showing any signs of doing it for a reason.

After a moment Justin too noticed the change and gradually uncurled. He pushed himself up from the ground and shook off the remaining rodents with a jerky dance of revulsion.

'That . . . was unpleasant,' he announced, to nobody in particular.

'You don't say.' Joy brushed herself down shakily and looked around.

What little snow had fallen here amongst the trees had all but vanished in the scrimmage, but the ground beneath was still damp and muddy from its passing. She could see marked out in the dirt the crude, shaky loop that Eilersen had drawn around the four of them. It was when the animals crossed that ragged demarcation line that they seemed to forget what they were doing. Already the rats were beginning to vanish into the woods and the birds to fly away, wariness of humans returning now that they were no longer under Dracherion's control.

'OK, what just happened here?' Justin asked. He was filthy and covered in scratches, and somewhat unsteady on his feet.

Eilersen smiled briefly. 'I made a magic circle.'

Justin staggered over to examine it. 'Looks like more of a' – he had to gasp for breath – 'more of a magic blob to me.'

Eilersen wiped mud from the edge of the pendant with the cloth he used to clean his glasses. 'I figured a big show of power like this must be stretching Dracherion's control pretty thin. So I gambled that using the protective magic of the necklace to draw a circle might be enough to break it.'

'Gambled. Oh, that's great,' Justin grumbled, but his heart clearly wasn't in it.

'You OK?' Joy asked him worriedly.

'Well, I'm not covered in *rats*,' he said. He glanced at the fourth member of their group, so far silent. 'Trev, you OK?'

Trevor jumped at the address. 'Oh, I, er, yeah. I'm fine,' he said, though he looked decidedly miserable.

'Great.' As usual, Justin missed the subtext entirely, or else was just too tired to bother taking

136

it at anything but face value. He yawned and gave a bone-cracking stretch. 'Right. What now?'

'Our house?' Joy suggested. All she wanted to do right now was stumble home, take a shower and some painkillers, and then sleep for a week.

'Not me.' They all turned to Eilersen with various levels of confusion or accusation, but he remained unmoved. 'My parents think it's wildly out of character enough that I stayed away last night; they'll be calling out search and rescue if I don't go home all weekend.'

'Assuming that's where you're *going*.' Justin curled his lip. 'Maybe you were the one creeping around scratching warnings into people's doors last night.'

'Maybe *you* were,' Eilersen countered. 'You left the room before I did.'

'Leaving *you* the perfect opportunity to sneak off.'

'Guys, give it break,' said Joy uneasily, cradling her injured wrist. 'We don't need to help Dracherion by fighting over stuff nobody can prove.'

'Yeah, well, we shouldn't help Dracherion by, oh, *helping Dracherion*, either,' Justin said sharply. 'We shouldn't split up. We've got to solve this!'

137

'Believe me, the last thing I want to do is leave you three alone where you can do something stupid,' Eilersen said as they limped back towards the gate, straightening clothing and assessing their injuries. 'But having my parents get so suspicious they start following me around to investigate isn't my idea of the best plan ever, either. We've caused enough trouble already without dragging innocent bystanders into it.'

Any budding retort was cut off as they emerged onto the road outside and found it still littered with dead birds. Joy had half expected them to have disappeared, but they remained, a stark reminder that Dracherion's powers were more than just illusion. As they limped back onto Llewellyn Road, they saw people coming out of their houses to puzzle over the carnage.

'So, what, we're just going to go home?' Justin demanded. 'Give up on any chance of catching Dracherion off-guard while it's recovering? This might be our best chance!'

'Catch it off guard with *what*?' Eilersen retorted. 'Hurtful sarcastic remarks? We don't have the first clue how to fight this thing! And we don't know how long it will need to recover – if it even does. The amount of blood that's been spilled today is only going to make it more powerful.'

Joy was suddenly twice as conscious of her bruised and battered body, relatively minor injuries taking on a grim new significance. Dracherion wasn't just kicking them around for the fun of it; every time it hurt them, it grew stronger.

'Which is exactly why we need to act now!' Justin shouted, drawing a disapproving look from a few people gathered across the street. 'We've been running around all day trying to find alternatives, but there *are* no alternatives! We're not going to find a handy cheat sheet somewhere called "How to Banish a Spirit Without Any Risks". The only way to fight it is with magic, and the only magic we've got is in the book. There must be *something* in one of the rituals that could help us. We've got to start taking some chances, or we're toast.'

'He's right,' Joy said. Eilersen gave her a disgusted look.

'*Thank* you.' Her brother folded his arms.

'But we can't do anything tonight,' she continued. She went on quickly before he could voice the inevitable protest. 'Justin, we're all half dead. Nobody's in any shape to try and do more magic. We're too tired, and we'll only screw it up. If Dracherion *is* temporarily weakened, then we need to use the time to rest, not go chasing after it without a proper plan.'

Her own energy seemed to have drained out of the soles of her feet, and Trevor looked sweaty and trembly. She was sure the only thing keeping Justin upright was sheer stubbornness. Trying to go on the attack tonight would be suicide. She couldn't even face the thought of walking her vandalized bike home. It could stay chained up with Justin's for another night.

'Tomorrow,' Eilersen said, nodding to himself. 'We'll rest, we'll meet up again, and then we're going to have to try *something*. Because if we don't, I don't think we're going to make it through Sunday alive.'

Despite Justin's continued grumbling, Eilersen
eventually split off from them to go home
alone. He handed the necklace back before
he left them, and Joy managed to fix the chain and
put it on. Even that tiny weight felt like a burden.

Her wrist, she had decided, was probably not
broken, although it still hurt like hell. Justin was staggering along like a drunk. Trevor twice offered to
take the weight of the book for him, but he refused
to hand it over.

'You'll have to let go of it sometime,' Joy pointed
out. His reluctance to part with it made her edgy,

though she knew it could be nothing more than caution. They didn't want the book to fall into the hands of whoever Dracherion had possessed. The trouble was, that person might be Justin. Neither he nor Eilersen had a watertight alibi for the previous night, and their mistrust of each other fed into her own.

'Hey, I fought off an army of rats for this book,' he said, more than half serious. 'I'm sleeping with it under my *pillow.*'

He looked as though he'd been through a war zone; they all did. Joy's hair was a literal rats' nest, and her hands and face were covered in scratches. She could only hope her parents would be out or busy, and they'd get a chance to clean up.

She'd forgotten her dad had been planning to fix the front door. He was tidying up in the front hall when they arrived, leaving them with no way to sneak in.

'Justin. Joy.' He regarded them levelly, sparing a small nod of acknowledgement for Trevor. This time, clearly, the presence of a visitor wasn't going to be enough to get them out of providing a proper explanation. Joy toed the ground awkwardly.

'Hi, Dad. Um . . . Joy's done her wrist in,' Justin

supplied quickly, while Trevor tried to disappear into the background. 'She came off her bike in the slush, and we had to get it out of the ditch.'

A typical Justin Blake cover story – trying to sound responsible, play for sympathy *and* pass the blame off onto her. Unfortunately, it didn't look like Dad completely bought it. He turned to look at her.

'Which wrist?' he asked, and she held it out for inspection. Her father examined it carefully, but even his light touch was enough to make her wince.

'Hmm. Well, it looks like you've just sprained it. Ask your mother for some ice to put on it. You're lucky you didn't—' He suddenly stopped dead in mid-sentence. 'Joy . . . where did you get this?' He reached out to touch the silver pendant hanging round her neck.

'Oh, it's . . .' She was flustered, unnerved by the intent focus. Her father had the same eyes as Grandpa and Justin, strikingly blue and extremely hard to out-stare. 'Grandpa Blake gave it to me years ago, remember?'

'I thought you'd lost it,' he said, not letting up on his scrutiny of her face.

'So did I! But I found it by accident – it was in a drawer in your workbench in the garage.' She frowned, her puzzlement over that much, at least, not feigned.

An odd look passed over her father's face, vanishing too soon for her to be sure she'd read it properly. 'Put some ice on that wrist,' he directed, and strode down the hallway.

Joy stared after him a moment, mouth agape.

'I think he *hid* it,' she said to Justin in amazement.

'What? Your necklace?' He looked dubious. 'Why would he do that?'

'Because it's magic. Or just because Grandpa gave it to me. But he *knew* it was in that workbench drawer, and he's not happy I found it.' She was partly outraged, but mostly just startled. She knew her dad disapproved of anything even vaguely occult, but to take and hide something her grandpa had given her as a gift . . .

Justin shook his head impatiently. 'You're losing it,' he told her. 'He was just surprised you'd found it, that's all.' He brushed past her into the house.

Joy followed the boys up the stairs. 'Justin! Come

on. You don't think that was just a little bit weird?'
It wasn't like their father to leave so abruptly in the
middle of telling them off. 'And come to think of it,
why don't *you* have any jewellery or anything from
Grandpa Blake? Why would he give me something
that protects from evil influences, but not you?'

'He gave me a ring once, I think.' Her brother
shrugged. 'It was shaped like a snake or a dragon or
something. But Mum and Dad wouldn't let me wear
it to school . . . I think I sold it to somebody in the
end. How was I supposed to know it was important?'

'You weren't . . . but I bet Dad did.'

Who knew how many other little gifts their father
had hidden, diverted or refused over the years?
Things that could have helped them, maybe even
saved their lives . . . And the worst thing was, he
probably honestly believed he was protecting them.

'I don't think he bought your cover story, either,'
Joy added as they reached the upstairs landing.

'Relax, OK?' Justin still refused to listen. 'Even if
he *does* think we're up to something – and he probably just figures it's doing stupid bike stunts or
something – he's not exactly going to think, *Oh, no,*

they're doing magic! is he? He doesn't even believe in it.' He bounded on ahead.

Joy was not nearly so sure. True, they'd always assumed that Dad thought all this occult stuff was crazy . . . but that was before they'd found out for themselves that it was entirely too real.

What if their father wasn't angry because he thought it was all lies and fantasy, but was scared because he knew that it wasn't?

After taking a hasty shower and putting on some fresh clothes Joy began to feel halfway human again, but she was also bone tired. The adrenaline of fear had well and truly worn off, and dinner was a battle between hunger and the exhaustion that threatened to drag her face down onto her plate. She was conscious of her father's eyes on them throughout the meal.

She remembered now the phone call that had come on Friday night. Perhaps Grandpa *did* have some kind of warning system that had told him something was up, and he'd called home to ask his son to check it out. Dad had been short and dismissive, as he always was when Grandpa tried to raise a topic he didn't like . . . but perhaps there was more to his reaction than just disbelief. Perhaps there always had been, and they just hadn't known enough to understand.

Justin's earlier questions about Dad's family suddenly seemed more important. Had he found some reason to think their long-dead grandmother had some connection with the occult? And where had he got the name Lilian? Maybe their father's silence about his family meant something.

Of course, she could hardly ask Dad about it. Instead, she took the opportunity to corner her mother in the kitchen after dinner, when Justin and Trevor had gone back upstairs.

'Mum, do you remember that family-tree project I did a while back?'

'Oh, hello, Joy – could you pass me that pen? Thank you. Yes, I remember.' Her mother was preoccupied making a shopping list, and didn't look up.

Joy hovered in the kitchen doorway, keeping a wary eye out for her father. 'Well, I was going to update it for the website we have to design for IT. I was just wondering if you knew a bit more about Dad's family, because he didn't really seem to want to say much when I asked before.'

Her mother paused in her writing and gave Joy a searching look over her glasses. 'Your father doesn't like to talk about his childhood,' she said. 'It wasn't a very happy time for him. I'm not sure I can help you all that much, but it's best that you don't ask him, anyway. What did you need to know?'

'I was wondering about Grandma. Do you know when she died? I'd like to try and have all the dates on this time.' That seemed like the safest first avenue of attack.

'Hmm.' Mum inspected the contents of a cupboard. 'Well, I couldn't tell you the exact date, but your father was . . . seventeen, perhaps? Yes, that sounds right. Before he started university, anyway, because that was where I met him.'

Joy was surprised. 'Really? I thought he was younger than that.' She'd assumed that he didn't remember his mother that well, since he so rarely mentioned her.

Her mum smiled slightly at that. 'Well, sweetheart, I'm sure *you* don't think so, but seventeen is really not that old. And just when you're about to start out on your own adult life is probably one of the worst times you can lose a parent, especially in such tragic circumstances.'

'How did she die?' Joy asked nervously.

Her mother hesitated for a moment, as if assessing exactly how much she should say. 'She drowned,' she said finally. 'The family was already going through some tough times, and your father and grandfather weren't able to lean on each other as much as they should to get through it. Your grandfather's a proud man, Joy. Kinder-hearted than your dad gives him credit for, but very stubborn. He's always had a strong personality, and he's used to other people rolling over and doing things his way.'

'Kind of like Justin,' Joy observed.

Her mother smiled, though she hadn't really meant it as a joke. 'Yes – and your father too, though he'd be appalled to hear it. He wouldn't accept an apology even if your grandfather knew how to make one. They have never sorted out their differences, although they've learned to at least try and put them aside for a while since you two were born.'

'But what did they argue about in the first place?' This part Joy thought she probably knew, but she wondered how much her mother could tell her. 'It must have been something pretty big.'

Her mum smiled rather sadly and shook her head. 'You'll learn soon enough, Joy, that it's not always a big drama. It's the little things, the daily grind that wears people down. Your Grandpa Blake is very devoted to some ideas that your father just doesn't agree with, and it's difficult for them to find any common ground without falling back into the same old arguments.'

It sounded plausible enough . . . but Joy didn't think that was anywhere near the whole story. For the second time in as many hours, she couldn't help but feel that one of her parents was hiding something from her.

'Anyway.' Her mother tapped her pen and moved on to investigate another cupboard. 'That's enough depressing family history for now, I think. Was there anything else you needed to know?'

She remembered she had one more card to play. 'Oh, just one thing,' Joy added, trying to sound as if it was a casual afterthought. 'Did Dad ever have a relative called Lilian?'

The smile abruptly slipped, and so did her mother's pen, sending a smear of black ink through the neatly printed list. 'Lilian?' she said, too carefully.

'Yeah. I'm sure I remember hearing somebody say something about—'

'It's a family name,' Mum said quickly, before Joy could finish. 'Passed down through the Blake family, just the same as Lucien. I should imagine your father had several relatives with that name – aunts or cousins and such. But please don't go asking him about it, because he doesn't—'

To Joy's great frustration, Justin came barging into the kitchen just then, ruining her chances of pressing for more. 'Hi, Mum. Oh, hey, Joy. Listen, is it all right if I stay over at Trevor's tonight?'

'I thought you were staying in?' Joy said, confused by his sudden switch. Hadn't Justin been the one preaching earlier that they should stick together?

'Change of plan,' he said, shrugging it off as if it was nothing. 'So, Mum, can I?'

'Of course, if it's all right with Mrs Somerville.

Do you need a lift?' Mum seemed thoroughly relieved to escape the previous conversation.

'No, it's all right. It's only a couple of streets – we can walk it. Thanks, Mum!' He breezed out.

Joy was momentarily torn, but the interruption had given her mother a chance to recover some composure. She doubted whether she would get any further with her questions now. 'Thanks for the help, Mum,' she said resignedly, and trailed after her brother.

'No problem, dear – but remember, don't bother your father with it,' her mother cautioned, sounding just a little desperate.

'I won't,' she promised. But for reasons other than preserving his peace of mind. She was now positive that whatever her parents were avoiding involved magic, Grandpa Blake and this mysterious Lilian.

But that wasn't her most immediate concern.

'Justin!' she hissed as she followed her brother out into the hall. 'I thought we were agreed we were going to stick *together* tonight?'

He paused and turned halfway up the stairs. 'Yeah, but we can't, can we? Dad's already annoyed that we brought Eilersen back without asking first yesterday.

He'd never let me have someone stay over tonight. And you know how freaked Trevor's going to get if we send him back home on his own.'

'Yeah, but what about *me*?' Joy wanted to demand, and didn't because it would sound pathetic. 'At least leave the book here,' she bargained. She couldn't help suspecting that his concern for Trevor's nerves was nothing but an excuse to sneak off and do something dangerous.

'Oh, no way!' Justin retorted instantly. 'It stays with me. And it's better that we keep the book and the necklace apart, so that Dracherion can't go after them both together.'

'Or better to keep them together, so the necklace can protect the book,' she countered.

He rolled his eyes. 'Look – Dracherion's bound to be resting up, just like we are. That big show in the park today *has* to have cost it something. I really don't see it making another attack on us tonight – and if we're not all bunched up in the same place, then it'll have an even harder time trying to take us out.'

'That's not what you were saying to Eilersen earlier,' she said suspiciously.

Justin glowered. 'Yeah, well, I don't like him being off on his own where none of us can watch him. He was pretty fast to make an excuse to get away. But this is OK. You've got the necklace for protection, and me and Trevor can keep an eye on each other. It's the smartest way for us to split up.'

'Justin . . .' Joy stopped him as he turned to go, but she couldn't think of a single argument that would stand a chance of getting through to him. 'Um . . . why were you asking about all Dad's family earlier?' she asked instead.

'Oh. No reason.' He shrugged and gave her a smile. 'I just came across some pictures at Grandpa's, that's all.'

'OK.'

But as he left her standing there on the stairs, Joy couldn't help but wonder.

Whenever Justin visited Trevor's house, he was struck all over again by how *grey* it was. It shouldn't be a surprise, but it was one of those things that always seemed over-exaggerated in hindsight, as if he was remembering it worse than it really was.

It was hard to say exactly what made the house so drab. It wasn't as if there was no colour – the carpet was deep red, and there were brightly coloured pictures on the walls – but there was an air of sad neglect about the place that dragged you down. Whenever he stepped inside, Justin had a disturbing urge to go on one of his mother's 'look at the *state* of this place!' cleaning sprees.

He didn't suppose it would matter if the Somervilles had been bright, bubbly people who gave the house its life, but they weren't. Mrs Somerville was as bland and as dull as her peeling wallpaper, and she shuffled around like a woman twice her age. She barely acknowledged Justin when he was there, and didn't seem to talk to Trevor at all except to snap at him.

All in all, Trevor's house was a place he usually avoided like the plague. Why had he decided to come here again?

'Justin?' Trevor glanced back at him after he paused for too long on the doorstep. His friend looked less edgy now, probably relieved to be back on his home turf. Justin had to admit, it was hard to imagine Dracherion attacking them here. The house seemed entirely too boring to allow it.

'Yeah, sorry. Zoning out.' He shook himself.

Of course, Mrs Somerville's lack of attention was exactly why they'd come here. He thought Joy was overreacting, but it *was* possible their dad suspected something. Best not to tempt fate by doing magic right under his nose. And Joy herself would only try to stall him. Didn't she realize there was no time to lose? They couldn't afford to let this wait until morning.

Trevor's room was at the back of the house, with a window that looked out over the scrappy little garden. It was a younger boy's room really: there was still a faded clown rug on the floor and curtains with pictures of aeroplanes. The walls were covered in posters for sci-fi movies, and stacks of comics and hand-labelled videos were scattered everywhere.

'OK,' said Justin, pulling the book out of his bag. 'There has to be an answer in here somewhere.'

He'd tried to study the book when he was at home, but a throbbing headache had made focus impossible. Now, though, the very first page he found in English led to inspiration.

'See?' he said aloud, more to himself than to Trevor. 'Get Eilersen off my back for ten seconds and I've already found something.'

He didn't remember even seeing this page before. And that was enough to make him suspicious. He and Eilersen had combed through the contents of this book over and over again. How could he have missed a spell that might be helpful to them?

Unless Eilersen had distracted him deliberately . . .

Deciding to press ahead with this tonight instead of waiting for the others might well have been a very smart move.

'What did you find?' Trevor asked, leaning over.

Justin allowed him a quick glimpse of the page. 'There's a spell here for making a magic mirror. It's harmless – it just shows you an image of whatever you want to see. Which means that instead of just guessing, we can *ask* it what we have to do to fix this. It's perfect.' He skimmed the instructions and looked up. 'OK. We need a mirror. Biggest one you can find.'

At least Trevor seemed to have grasped the gravity of their situation, for he moved to obey without any of his usual hesitancy. 'What about a silver tray?' he suggested. 'There's one in the kitchen.'

'Great. In fact, can you fill it with water? Cover all the bases.' The ritual called for either a mirror or a basin of water, so it couldn't hurt to combine the two.

'I'll get it.' Trevor headed for the door.

Justin stood up and looked around the room. Despite Trevor's assurances, he wasn't totally convinced Mrs Somerville would stay oblivious; they might need to hide the evidence quickly. He decided to roll the rug back, so any signs of their working could be covered with it afterwards.

There turned out to be an unforeseen problem with that plan: Trevor's rug already *had* a magic circle underneath it.

Justin stared at the chalked design in stupefaction. It was not the same as the one they'd used the day before, but it looked very nearly as complicated. It consisted of a pair of nested circles, the band between them filled with writing in an unknown alphabet. The chalk had been smeared somewhat by the heavy rug, but what he could see certainly looked genuine.

What was it meant to do? And, more importantly, what was it doing on Trevor's floor?

As he peered closer, Justin noticed that there was a faint black scar on the floorboards towards the middle of the circle. It was hard to tell if it was a burn, a smear of dirt or just an ill-judged brushstroke in the woodstain. He reached out to see if he could rub it away with his thumb.

There was a whisper of sound from behind him. Justin whirled, hand going to his chest as his heart tried to make a break for it. For a moment the shape in the doorway was a hulking, menacing shadow . . . and then it was just Trevor.

'Sorry.' Trevor winced apologetically, although for a second Justin thought he saw a smirk. He sat back, feeling stupid for being so spooked. He must have been really far out of it if he'd failed to hear Trevor coming.

'Sorry,' Trevor said again. He was carrying a round metal serving tray with a gravy jug full of water on it; he set it down carefully on the bed, still managing to spill some. 'Oh, you found . . . Yeah,' he mumbled as he saw what Justin had uncovered.

Justin pointed down at the circle and raised an enquiring eyebrow. 'New home-decorating trend?'

Trevor set his jaw in an odd mix of embarrassment and defiance. 'I just thought maybe that if I had some kind of circle here, Dracherion might be less likely to—'

'Good thought,' Justin said kindly, although privately he suspected that it wouldn't have done Trevor much good unless he'd spent the whole night sitting in it. Of course, for all he knew, Trevor might well have. 'Where did you get the design?' he asked.

'Just off the Internet. I don't even know if it's real.' As usual, Trevor tried his hardest to dismiss his own ideas as pathetic before anyone else had a chance to do so. Justin found it both sad and rather frustrating – after all, it wasn't as if the rest of them had taken any better precautions. Worst-case scenario, it would have just been useless, and there was no saying it *hadn't* saved Trevor from a nasty midnight visitation.

'Wish I'd thought of that,' he said loyally. 'Might have stopped Eilersen throwing a hissy fit in the middle of the night just because I got up for a glass of water. Didn't get any visitors, did you?' he asked, indicating the possible scorch mark and not one hundred per cent joking.

Trevor ducked his head sheepishly. 'Oh. No. I just, um, I knocked over a candle.'

Justin laughed and felt his chest begin to unknot a little. 'Yeah, well, least you didn't burn the house down. Come on, let's have a look at this magic mirror.'

The tray was, on closer examination, not quite burnished enough to produce a good reflection, but since he was going to be enchanting it, not doing his hair, Justin didn't think that was important. There were hand gestures and words to recite as he poured in a thin layer of water, and he copied them all conscientiously. He could be precise and cautious when it counted; that was what the others didn't understand. Last night had been an accident, an aberration. If he'd known from the start that it was going to be so dangerous, he would have been a lot more careful.

'A clockwise turn . . . touch your head, your eyes and your heart with your left hand, then draw the symbols on the surface of the water . . .'

Justin followed Trevor's carefully read directions. 'Writing' with the index finger of his left hand was awkward, and it made the cut across his palm ache fiercely. He worried for a moment that it would split open again, but the rigid demands of the ritual soon washed it from his mind. There was something exhilarating but also soothing about going through the motions, building magic step by step from mundane actions. Not difficult, but *secret*: knowledge given to only a few.

'Now the candles . . .'

Trevor switched off the lights, and the shallow tray of water became a dark, inky pool that could have been deep beyond imagining. Justin scraped a match along the packet, the tiny flame that sprang up turning the ripples to lines of fire. He lit six candles one by one and set them in a ring around the tray, aware of a faint whisper in the air despite the stillness of the room.

Or perhaps it was the blood rushing in his ears. He was hyper-aware of his own pulse, no longer panicky but a strong, solid thump that reverberated through him. He could feel every beat in the wound on his left palm.

'Good.' Trevor looked strange in the candlelight, his normal ruddy pink complexion all stark highlights and deep shadow. As he dipped his head to look at the next page of the book, his face took on the lines of a skull. 'Now place your left hand in the centre of the mirror and speak the words.'

Justin reached out and touched . . . nothing. Not water, not simply empty air, but a coldness that seeped into the pads of his fingers and numbed him all the way up to his elbow. He was sure that if he pushed his hand down further, it would still meet no resistance, just keep going . . . and then the rest of him would tumble down into the darkness after it, frozen solid.

He closed his eyes, and the words were there as vividly as the candle flames. Not just remembered but recognized, as if some part of him had already been aware of what he needed to say. They spilled from his tongue smoothly, impossible to stop in mid-flow even if he'd wanted to.

'Mirror, by the powers thus invoked, I command thee: do my bidding. Show the scenes that I request, without falsehood or deception; make response with speed and clarity, and discharge all power when I bid thee end thy service. So I command!'

With a blast of chilled air as if from an open freezer door, the mirror came to life.

Justin opened his eyes to find the room aglow with shimmering light. The magic mirror had turned to quicksilver, slick and shining, and rippled like the surface of a lake in a high wind. The waves travelled across its surface slowly, but there was a mind-blowing impression of size, as if he was looking at a much larger image zoomed out until it fitted the space.

The candles had all been snuffed out; their illumination wasn't missed. The light from the mirror was as bright as midday sunshine, but far colder, with the bleached-out silver quality of moonlight.

'It worked.' Justin smiled in triumph. It was no longer quite so startling to see magic in action, but working it himself still came with an overwhelming burst of pride. He was sure he could cast spells until he was a hundred and twelve and never, ever get tired of that exultant flare of *I did that*.

But first things first. 'Test it,' urged Trevor, gazing at their handiwork with an expression that was somewhere between hunger and pride.

Trevor understood what they had here. He wasn't like the others – they were too obsessed with the risks to even realize what they could do. This was *power*: power in its purest, most untainted form, much greater than anything you could achieve using physical or mechanical strength. It was theirs for the taking, and they could do *anything* with it.

Justin massaged his left arm, still numb to the point of deadness. He saw the potential in this, but he wasn't stupid; there *were* dangers, and he didn't plan to blithely skip ahead without a thought for any of them. He intended to test the mirror in a completely harmless way before he even dreamed of relying on it for their salvation.

A smirk curved the corners of his mouth as the perfect idea came to him.

'Mirror, show me,' he said precisely, 'the teenage boy that I know by the name of Daniel Eilersen, as he is right now, without any kind of trickery or mis-representation. If this duty cannot be discharged as I describe, then tell me, and tell me why, and do so without delay or omission of any detail.'

There. No loopholes.

The mirror went dark . . . and stayed dark. Justin waited, and waited, and his heart started to clench with the horrible aching fear that it had all gone wrong *again* . . . and then realization dawned. He chuckled nervously and smacked his forehead with the heel of his good hand.

'Duh. Um . . . Mirror, show me the scene that I requested, but lit as if it was daylight.' Covering all the loopholes was still no substitute for common sense. Which was exactly why a safe first test had been a good idea.

The image immediately brightened and developed into a dim picture rather like CCTV footage, albeit still distorted by that rolling ripple. It showed Eilersen under a black and grey duvet, apparently deeply asleep. That was all it displayed – the space where the rest of the room should have been was fogged over. The magic mirror was no camera, but showed only what it was directed to. There could have been a mad axeman poised over the sleeping boy ready to strike, and his magical observers wouldn't have known it.

Asleep, he did look like a boy; younger than his fifteen years – never mind the middle-aged man he often seemed, with his finicky, pretentious attitude. He looked paler and skinnier than ever against the dark sheets, and his face was oddly naked without his glasses. Justin felt an unanticipated pang of guilt for spying on him, and quickly stamped it down.

'Cute pyjamas,' he mocked instead, and waved a hand over the surface of the magic mirror. 'OK. Clear that image.' He glanced across at Trevor. 'What now?'

'Ask it if there's anything in your grandfather's house that can make us more powerful,' Trevor suggested, leaning forward eagerly.

Justin frowned slightly. It was good idea, but they

should probably word it a bit more carefully. He wasn't sure if the mirror was as inclined to trickery as Dracherion had been, but best not to give it any openings for misinterpreting their questions. He composed the next question in his head.

'Mirror: show us any and all artefacts or papers in the house of Lucien Blake that would be useful to us against the spirit called Dracherion.'

The mirror . . . pulsed. He wasn't sure exactly what it was doing, but he had a hunch it was the equivalent of TV static, or the fatal-error blue screen on a computer. A succession of images seemed to half form but fragment before they became fully visible. The silver glow radiating out from the mirror flickered crazily.

'Crap! Why's it doing that?' He cringed backwards, half fearful that it would explode or do something worse from the overload. 'Clear! Clear!' He waved a hand frantically until the chaotic mess disappeared.

'Maybe it means that Dracherion *can't* be defeated,' said Trevor. He sounded unsurprised, barely even resigned – as if he'd suspected as much all along.

Justin wouldn't believe it. 'Or we just didn't ask

the right question. Maybe there were too many things for it to show at once . . . or it's not smart enough to distinguish between useful and "could, conceivably, be a tiny bit of help if you did something crazy with it" . . .'

He needed to *think*, and that was getting hard. His head was pounding . . . or was the sensation coming from his hand? He was still getting funny signals from it where the numbness was slow to recede, and when he looked at his palm, blood was seeping once more from the knife wound. In the silvery light it looked almost unreal, more like droplets of molten metal.

Trevor was talking, and he'd been in a daze. 'What? Sorry?'

'I said, you've got to admit it's possible, Justin. There's no reason to believe we *can* defeat this thing – it's so powerful . . . It might not be too late to try and strike a bargain.' He sounded earnest, but Justin thought there was a spark of panic in his eyes, as if he was equally afraid that Justin might agree as that he wouldn't.

'Forget it!' he said emphatically. He refused to even entertain the idea of surrendering. Once you started obsessing over all the reasons why things were hope-less, it became a self-fulfilling prophecy. There *was* a way out of this. There had to be. And he would find it . . . if only he could start thinking clearly again.

'Then we should use the mirror to spy on Dracherion,' Trevor urged. 'Use it defensively, to see if any of us are in danger. We can't fight, but we can try to protect ourselves . . .'

'I'm not done yet!' Justin insisted, although his head was splitting. There had to be something else he could try, some different angle that would show the solution to him. 'Mirror, show me . . . show me why the spirit that calls itself Dracherion wanted this book.'

He'd expected – hoped – that it would show him one of the pages, tell them which ritual Dracherion didn't want them to perform. Instead, as the glow of the mirror shrank down to a pinpoint and then re-expanded, he saw the book lying in the centre of a ring of candles. There were hands pressing down on it – three pairs? four pairs? – but it was difficult to see them, because the book was glowing—

Except *glowing* wasn't quite the right word, because instead of light the book was exuding darkness: a cloud of blackness that looked like it must be poisonous, corrosive, some form of deadly radiation made visible. And then, finally, the darkness shrank down, and the book was just a book again. It was lifted by one of the pairs of hands, and as the eye of the magic mirror drew back, Justin could see that they belonged to his grandfather. The Lucien Blake of the photos, a man to whom grandchildren were still a thought for the distant future. Despite the years between, he didn't look much younger; his hair was red instead of white, but the lines on his face were already drawn deep by stress and worry.

Justin wanted to see who the rest of the ritual-workers were, but the mirror did not oblige him. Instead, he saw his grandfather carry the book over to what looked to be the same wooden chest where Justin had found it, wrap it up and lock it away. Then the vision faded.

'They did something to the book,' he realized aloud. 'It's not about the spells at all; they actually put something in it. Some kind of energy . . . ?'

'Dracherion's energy.' Trevor spoke up suddenly. 'They must have trapped it inside the book somehow.

Maybe there's still some power left in the book that it wants to get at – or else it just doesn't want to risk that happening again.'

Justin groaned and rubbed his face. 'So the answer's *not* in any of the rituals after all. Dracherion just wants the book for its own reasons.'

Despite his earlier vow, a wave of crushing despair threatened to break over him. Maybe there *was* no way to get out of this. He'd hoped that something in the book might be their secret weapon, but now it seemed that keeping it out of Dracherion's grasp had only been delaying the inevitable. They could only run and hide a little longer.

No. There *had* to be a way to fight back.

'What we *really* need,' said Trevor pensively, 'is Dracherion's real name. If we had that, we could have control of the spirit whether it was free or not.'

Justin sat up abruptly. 'Can we *ask* that?' he wondered, startled. The mirror was supposed to be able to show them anything. Could it really be that simple?

'We can try,' said Trevor, sounding bold although his eyes were frightened.

Justin drew himself up, feeling a little bit of hope

return to his battered and aching body. 'Mirror,' he said, clearly and firmly, 'show me Dracherion's true name.'

There was a violent cracking sound, and the mirror went dark. So did everything else.

'Justin. Justin? Justin . . .'

Consciousness returned gradually, but not gently; it was like having the covers dragged off when he was trying very hard to stay asleep. Justin didn't want to open his eyes, let alone get up, but his body's signals of discomfort were getting louder and louder. His insides felt dried out and raw, like an all-over sore throat.

At some point the lights had come back on. Trevor was pressed up against the far wall, staring at him warily. Something in his expression made Justin hesitate to complete his push to stand up.

'What?' he said nervously.

The room was in disarray. Their candles had been knocked over – thankfully, none of them still alight – and the silver tray appeared to have shattered into pieces. If there had been water left in it to spill, it had since dried up or been mopped away. There was a dark stain on the rolled-up carpet under his hand, and he realized it was blood. His own, he guessed. The cut on his palm was no longer bleeding, but it looked red and sore, as if it might be infected.

'Are you . . . OK?' Trevor asked him.

Justin was pretty sure that a thumping headache and the sick taste in his mouth weren't quite what he was interested in. 'Yeah . . . I think so . . .'

'What's the last thing you remember?'

Justin struggled, finding the memories difficult to pull together. His thoughts seemed slow and viscous, like thick treacle oozing along. 'I . . . I asked the mirror about Dracherion's name. And then . . . I guess it broke or something. It all went dark. Did I pass out?'

Trevor continued to stare at him. 'You really don't remember anything after that?'

'After what? It was just a second ago.' He realized that was wrong immediately: the room hadn't got like this in a few moments. He swallowed nervously. 'Feels like it, anyway. How long have I been out?'

'You've been unconscious for nearly an hour. But you were awake before that.'

'Well, *obv*—' Justin bit back the automatic sardonic retort. There was something else here, something important that he wasn't understanding. 'What do you mean?' he asked instead.

His old friend was still keeping well away from him, as if he might snap or lunge at any moment. 'I mean, you didn't pass out, Justin. Not then, anyway. There was more before that happened.'

Justin blinked at him in utter bafflement, a shiver crawling across his skin. He remembered no such thing, and he wanted to deny it, but the fearful look in Trevor's eyes kept him silent. It ran a lot deeper and darker than the usual anxious insecurity. He looked in fear for his very life.

'I *really* don't remember anything,' Justin insisted. 'What did I do?'

'I don't think it was you,' said Trevor grimly, and

a strange look flitted briefly across his face. 'It was
. . . I don't know, but it didn't seem like you. It
didn't . . . it didn't *move* right.'

Justin tried to suppress a shudder. It sounded like
Trevor was suggesting . . .

'Tell me exactly what happened,' he said tightly.
'Right from the start.'

Trevor shifted position, stretching his legs out as if
he'd been sitting cramped up in the same place for
a long time. He looked almost shamefaced, as if he
was afraid to say something Justin would take badly.

'Well, at first, um . . . nothing happened,' he began,
the words coming in disjointed bursts. 'The mirror
went dark again, like it did when you asked it to show
Eilersen, and I heard it crack. But then we just sat
there for a while. I was waiting for you to do something, but you were kind of in a trance or something
– you were like that earlier too . . .'

'I had a headache.' 'Had' was probably the wrong
word. The heavy bass-drum thump had become
more of a dull ache, but it had settled in around his
temples and wasn't going anywhere.

'Yeah. So I waited a while, and I figured the mirror

wasn't going to do anything, so I asked you if you were going to cancel it, but you didn't answer me. I kept talking, and it was like you didn't even know I was there. And' – he looked sheepish – 'I got a bit freaked out, so I got up and turned on the lights.'

Trevor stared at his hands. 'You were just . . . sitting there. Looking at nothing. And then you got up, but it was . . . weird. Like watching a puppet, or like somebody was picking you up and moving you around instead of you moving yourself. I thought you were going to—'

He licked his lips nervously and didn't finish, but he didn't need to. Justin could imagine only too well what Trevor must have been thinking. Because while he might well have blanked out on a few minutes of sitting and vegetating, he was damn sure he hadn't got up and walked about.

And that meant that while he was unconscious, something else *had*.

'So I got up, and I was' – Trevor ducked his head, ashamed of himself – 'I was moving towards the door . . .'

'It's OK,' Justin said quietly. Only Trevor would

be mentally beating himself up for running away when his best friend was acting like an extra from *Dawn of the Dead*.

Trevor flinched. 'I was headed towards the door,' he repeated, 'and then you – it – it just moved really *fast*, and it grabbed me, and' – he looked mortified – 'I think I fainted. Or – or maybe it did something to me, I don't know. But I blacked out, and when I woke up a few minutes later, you were already, um . . . you were sleeping. And the room was like this. I didn't want to risk going near you, in case . . .'

'Yeah. I get it,' Justin said. His own voice sounded rough and alien to his ears. Suddenly everything *felt* alien, used, like he'd pulled on somebody else's dirty clothes. Dracherion had taken control of his body, possessed it, moved him around as easily as it had the birds and rats.

Moved him around to do . . . what, exactly?

He rocked upright, causing Trevor to shrink back in alarm.

'What did it *want*?' Justin asked aloud. 'If it took me over, and it didn't do anything to you except maybe knock you out, then what did it *want*?'

'Maybe it was just seeing if it could,' Trevor offered anxiously. He made no move to come out of his corner; indeed pressed further back into it.

'Maybe,' Justin conceded, but he didn't believe it. Because if Dracherion had truly taken possession of his body, this was almost certainly not the first time.

A sick chill slunk down his back as he remembered the early hours of the morning before. He'd told Joy and Eilersen that he'd gone for a glass of water, but actually he'd been driven out of bed by his hand beginning to bleed. And when he reached the kitchen, he'd felt so dizzy he'd had to sit down . . .

His memory insisted that he'd only sat there for a matter of minutes – but how could he be sure? If he'd had a total blackout just now, there was no way of guaranteeing he hadn't had others. Maybe it *had* been him who'd gone out and scratched those symbols on the doors, returned to the park to clean up the debris of their ritual and left the front door open. He'd woken up the next day with a body racked by aches and pains that he had no better explanation for.

'The book!' Justin suddenly remembered it and

hurried to rifle through the disordered contents of the room. What if it was gone? What if Dracherion had destroyed it, or—?

It was under the bed. The sight of it was such a profound relief that Justin found himself bizarrely close to bursting into tears. He crawled beneath the bed to retrieve it, grateful that the dust gave him the excuse to cough any embarrassing traces away.

He needed to *sleep*, he knew, and quite desperately. His brain and body had used up more than the last of their reserves, and if he didn't get some proper rest soon, he was about to have some sort of melt-down. But right now the thought of even closing his eyes was truly horrifying. If he temporarily surrendered his consciousness, who knew what might wake up in his place?

The book was reassuringly intact and solid in his hands as he sat down on the bed. The leather binding seemed warm to the touch, but that could be anything. Hot water pipes under the floor, or simply his imagination.

But *that* wasn't. Justin's breath caught in his throat as he saw that the zigzag Y of Dracherion's symbol had been burned into the covers. He reached out to touch it with his injured hand, and felt a brief shock, like static electricity. The inner pages of the book seemed to be unharmed, but that symbol was as good as the spirit being here in person to laugh mockingly.

Trevor met his eyes, and they shared a moment of silent horror.

What did it mean? Was it just another warning, like the markings on the doors? Dracherion had been able to get at the book, but it hadn't made any attempt to destroy it. Was that the spirit's way of saying that it didn't need to; the book was no threat to it?

Or was it something to do with the vision he'd seen in the mirror? Maybe Trevor was right, and some of Dracherion's power had still been locked up in the book. If the spirit had somehow reabsorbed it, then it could be stronger than ever.

'What do you think it means?' Trevor asked tentatively.

Justin could only shake his head, his reaction numbed by tiredness. 'I don't know. But whatever it is, we can't let Dracherion intimidate us. We've got to keep on fighting back.'

Somehow. Tomorrow. When his brain was working at full speed again.

But first they had to survive the night. 'We should get some sleep,' he said, and Trevor nodded, although neither of them made any move to get more comfortable. There was a spare mattress Justin usually slept on, but he couldn't summon the energy to get up and fetch it.

Eventually he groaned and lay back. Weariness tugged, but every time he started to nod off he kept jerking himself out of it. Dracherion might return at any moment, and he was afraid to sleep. How could he fight back if the spirit took over his mind while he was dead to the world?

Trevor eventually got into bed, but he stayed sitting up with the covers bunched around him, watching Justin with sharp and wary eyes.

It promised to be a long and uncomfortable night.

J oy woke at a quarter past seven, budding anxiety pushing her out of bed before she'd even remembered why. She didn't feel remotely rested, but with the threat of Dracherion hanging over them, the idea of trying to snatch more sleep seemed ludicrous. She was gripped by a frantic need to be *doing* something.

She just didn't have a clue what.

She wanted to call her brother, but it was too early for him to be awake, and he'd probably sleep right through his mobile's ringtone. Besides, what if her suspicions about the previous night were right? It could be safer not to try and contact him.

Joy dressed and ate breakfast, but her stomach was churning so badly she could barely keep the food down. She was too agitated to sit still; being this isolated and out of the loop was somehow even worse than being in the thick of things.

It was no good. She had to talk to someone or she would go insane.

There was only one Eilersen in the phone book, so she took a chance and dialled. The phone was picked up on the second ring.

'Hello?' Joy was taken aback by the cheerful singsong that greeted her. It was a male voice, but most definitely not Eilersen's.

'Er . . . hello. Can I speak to Daniel, please?'

'Of course you can. One moment.' The voice moved away from the receiver, but was still clearly audible as it switched to a bellow. 'Danny! Phone!'

There was a pause, then a click-clunk and a muffled: 'I've got it. Hello?'

'*Danny?*' Joy said sceptically, raising her eyebrows even though he couldn't see her.

'Only to my father,' he said, in a voice that promised dire reprisals for anyone who tried otherwise. 'What's going on?'

'I have no idea,' she said grimly. 'First chance he got, Justin ditched me to go over to Trevor's last night. They took the book with them.'

'So much for "we shouldn't split up".' She didn't need to see Eilersen to imagine the eye-roll. 'You realize he's just gone off to do something stupid as soon as we're not watching him?'

'There's Trevor,' Joy said, but not very confidently.

Eilersen snorted. 'Oh, please. Trevor wouldn't dare to tell him if he was wearing his pants outside his trousers.'

'Oh, come on. Trevor's shy, but he wouldn't let him do anything *crazy*,' she protested, made extra defensive by the sharp thread of guilt. Had she made a huge mistake, letting Justin go off alone with Trevor? But then again, how could she have stopped him?

'What makes you think he'd even get a vote?' Eilersen retorted. 'Your brother doesn't notice other people have opinions unless they're screaming them

187

at the top of their lungs. And even then he just bugs them until they give up and do what he wants.'

Guilt made her take that as a jab at her own ready compliance. 'Yeah, well, even if Justin has got the wrong idea, he's right that we've got to do something,' she said sullenly. 'We can't just sit and wait for Dracherion to come and get us.'

'Is there any chance your parents could help us?' Eilersen asked.

It was Joy's turn to snort rudely. 'Um, *no*. My dad's insanely anti-occult – in fact I think he actually must have *hidden* my necklace where we found it. If we told him what's going on, he might just confiscate all the stuff and stop us from trying to do anything.'

'Yes, because "La la la, I can't hear you" always works *so* well on homicidal evil spirits,' he said dryly. 'Do you think he knows your grandfather's magic is genuine?'

'I'm beginning to think so.' And she should have thought of it far earlier, but it was hard to step outside and look at patterns that had been part of her family history for as long as she could remember. 'I think it might involve my grandma and maybe the whole of the Blake side of the family, but nobody will tell me anything.'

'Maybe we should go back to your grandfather's and have another look around,' Eilersen suggested. 'There might be something important that we missed. And it's not as if we have any better leads. Have you got my address? You might as well meet me here – it's on your way.'

'OK. I'll see you soon.'

Joy felt a bit guilty to be cutting Justin and Trevor out of the loop, but it was a relief to have some kind of plan of action. She grabbed the key out of the kitchen, glad that Justin had remembered to return it, and was just sliding the phone book back into place when her father came downstairs.

'Joy? What are you doing up this early?'

'Dad! Oh. I was just looking up my friend's phone number – we've arranged to meet up in a bit. I was just leaving.' She was aware that she was babbling too much, trying to blurt it all out before he could frame awkward questions.

Her father sighed, and suddenly looked tired. 'Joy . . . what's going on?'

'What's going on what?' she asked, heart racing.

'I know you and your brother are up to something. You've been acting strangely all weekend, you're coming home injured—'

'I just sprained my wrist,' she interrupted defensively. It was a perfectly ordinary injury, the kind of thing she'd done dozens of times before. Her father had no reason to be suspicious if she didn't give it to him.

Joy knew she ought to meet his eyes to sell the words convincingly, but it was difficult when he looked more hurt and worried than angry.

'Joy, we're your parents,' he said, rubbing his face. 'We're here to *protect* you, not punish you. I know you don't want to get your brother in trouble, but if the two of you are in any kind of difficulty with – with anything, you *know* you can talk to us—'

To her dismay, Joy felt the hot prickle of tears wanting to well up, and quickly turned round again, taking refuge in straightening up the spines of the books. 'We *would*, Dad,' she insisted. 'If we were in trouble, we'd ask you for help.'

Just . . . not *this* kind of trouble. Her parents *couldn't* help, that was the thing. And involving them would only put their lives in danger too. She hated lying to either of them, but it wasn't for her own benefit or just for the sake of getting away with it. She and Justin had got themselves into this mess, and whether they could get themselves out she didn't know, but they weren't about to drag anybody else in if she could possibly help it.

'OK,' he said softly, sounding defeated. 'But whatever you're doing, just be careful, all right?'

'I will,' she promised. 'Bye, Dad.'

'Goodbye, Joy.'

She left him standing alone in the sunlit hallway, looking depressed.

There were few cars on the road at this time on a Sunday, and even fewer pedestrians. It was a little too eerie for comfort; not quite the snowbound stillness of the early hours of Saturday, but close to it. Her own footsteps echoed far too loudly, and every glimpsed flicker of movement had her jumping.

Eilersen's house wasn't what she'd expected, though she wasn't quite sure she could have said what that was. A building as neat and precise as he was, perhaps, instead of this slightly beaten-up old place with a garden full of flowers.

Her knock was quickly answered by a pretty, short-haired blonde woman in jeans and a knitted jumper. She looked rather curious about Joy's presence, but smiled pleasantly enough. 'Hi.'

'Hi, I'm sorry to call so early – um, is Daniel in?'

The inquisitive expression only grew. 'Well, yes, he is . . . Oh, please, come on in, you must be freezing out there. You're one of Daniel's school friends?'

'Er, yeah.' It seemed easiest. 'I'm Joy Blake.'

'Ah, the young lady who called earlier.' Eilersen's father appeared from the front room, carrying a newspaper. He was a big bear of a man, neither as fine-boned nor as reserved as his son, but somehow she could see something of Eilersen in him.

'Yeah. I'm really sorry to show up so early, but . . . really bad algebra crisis.' She smiled nervously.

Mr Eilersen grinned back. 'Of course. Well, that's definitely Danny's department. Just go on through, it's upstairs on the left. Don't worry, he's up – he's got his nose glued to the computer.'

The Eilersens seemed pleasant enough, if rather

surprised to see her; Eilersen's famous avoidance of a social life was obviously not exaggerated. She scurried through the house, feeling intrusive despite the invitation.

Eilersen barely pulled his gaze away from his computer screen to acknowledge her. 'Joy.' Even on a Sunday morning in his own bedroom he was neatly turned out, dark blue shirt buttoned all the way to the collar and at the cuffs. 'I was just trying to do some research into spirit possession.'

Possession. She couldn't help but shudder at the thought. 'Anything useful?'

He grimaced. 'Not really. The Internet's not exactly a trustworthy source in the first place, but in any case, everybody seems to agree that once a spirit has found a way to get into somebody's mind, there's very little you can do to stop it coming back.'

'And we know that it's found its way in.' One of them had already been possessed; Dracherion had left its calling card on their doors to make sure they knew as much. Now that it had figured out how to take control of its victim, it could come back and do it again any time it wanted.

And they still didn't know who its target was.

A thought had suddenly struck her. 'Hey . . . how come there's nothing carved on *your* front door?'

'Interesting, huh?' He gave her a sidelong look as he reached forward to turn off the monitor. 'Suggests that the person doing the carving knew where you and Trevor lived, but not where I do.'

'Or that it was you,' she countered, before she had time to think how unwise that was.

But Eilersen just smiled thinly. 'True. We shouldn't rule anybody out. I mean, *I* don't think it was me – although you only have my word for that – but if I was under Dracherion's control, there's no guarantee I would remember.'

'What makes you so sure it was one of us?' Joy asked, uncomfortable. It was a deeply creepy thought: not just that Dracherion might have taken control of one of them, but that whoever it was might not even know about it. 'I mean, it managed to take control of the birds without having any kind of special link to them.'

'Birds aren't people. And that wasn't exactly fine-tuned control. If it was that easy for Dracherion to waltz in and take over a human mind, it would have possessed a random body and killed us all already. No, I think it's got to work its way in gradually, looking for weaknesses.'

'What kind of weaknesses?'

Eilersen shrugged theatrically. 'I don't know why you're expecting that I'd know. Mental weaknesses, at a guess – doubts or overconfidence or . . . I don't know. It's not like I can get all this off the Internet.' He rose to get his coat. 'I'm just hoping your grandfather's library can tell us more than I found out yesterday.'

He didn't say anything else as they left the house, but Joy was sure she knew what he was thinking. If Dracherion had been probing for weaknesses through their ritually created connection . . . well, one of them was more connected than the others.

Joy thought of Justin, blearily stumbling about in the early hours of Saturday morning. Just getting a glass of water . . . or just returned from a far more sinister errand? If Eilersen was right about this, and she'd let Justin go off with the book . . .

If Eilersen was right. If Eilersen wasn't lying to her. If *he* wasn't the one under Dracherion's command.

All of a sudden she couldn't help thinking that going off alone with him might not be the wisest decision she'd ever made.

'So, er . . . your parents are nice,' she said inanely, trying to distract herself.

Eilersen smirked. 'No need to sound so surprised. What, you were looking for the horrible tragic secret that made me how I am today?'

Joy squirmed. 'I didn't say that.'

'You didn't need to. I could hear you thinking it.' He rolled his eyes. 'But if you're looking for some hidden torment Dracherion can use as a way in, look somewhere else. Some people are loners by choice, you know. I *like* being alone. I hate *not* being alone. And I'm not remotely miserable.'

'OK, OK!' Joy held up her hands in surrender. 'Solitude good. I get it.'

'Yes, well, you'd be amazed how many people don't.' Eilersen shook his head. 'I don't even want to know what my parents must be thinking about all this. Sleepovers, out for days in a row, visitors . . .'

'Well, it won't be for much longer, will it?' she said, and then regretted it.

'No,' he said soberly after a moment. 'No, one way or another, it won't.'

They walked faster.

XVII

When Joy was a little girl, her grandpa's study had seemed huge, like some legendary hall of magic treasures. As she'd grown older, it had turned into an ordinary room, not much bigger than her bedroom. Looking at it now, however, it seemed to have swelled back to its previous dimensions. How were they ever supposed to find anything in all this chaos?

'You and Trevor already went through all this yesterday?' she asked Eilersen.

'Well, *I* did. Trevor helped with the books, but he was reluctant to touch most of the rest of it.'

'Can't say I blame him,' Joy said with a shudder. Her grandfather's collection had been creepy in a cool way when they'd thought the occult artefacts were just curios. Now it was creepy in a 'who knows *what* it might do if you touch it?' way.

But they had to keep looking. She took a deep breath. 'OK. I'll take this bookshelf here. You start in that corner.'

She moved towards the shelves, but she hadn't even had time to pull down the first book when a faint sound came from the front of the house. They both froze.

Justin? Eilersen mouthed, meeting her eyes warily. She mutely shook her head, holding up the door key. Her brother wouldn't have come here if he knew he couldn't get in.

If he was acting of his own volition, of course.

There was another very soft sound, the tiny click of a door being closed by someone who was careful to muffle it. Heart racing, Joy took a slow step sideways and eased the desk drawer open, reaching in for the ceremonial knife. It wouldn't do much good against Dracherion and she certainly couldn't imagine using it against a person, but she thought she might feel safer if she was holding it.

It wasn't there.

Joy exchanged a panicked glance with Eilersen. She'd watched Justin put that knife back when they came here yesterday. If it wasn't there now, then one of the boys must have snuck it out.

Any one of the boys. She pressed herself into the corner by the door, attention flickering frantically between watching Eilersen and listening for the unknown intruder. Which one was the distraction, and which the danger?

Quiet footsteps drew closer, and they both tensed, ready, for better or worse, to leap first and ask questions later. If the intruder was some puppet of Dracherion's, there would be no second chances once the spirit realized they were onto it.

The footsteps approached the study door . . .

But they didn't come in. There was a sudden flood of fluid, alien words from the hallway outside, and the room exploded with a flare of brilliant light. Joy cried out and shielded her face, waiting for the roar of flames that would surely roast her alive.

Instead she heard, in tones of incredulity, '*Joy?*'

It was her grandfather's voice.

'Grandpa!'

She was utterly blinded by the flash, eyes glowing with multi-coloured afterimages. She staggered and collided with what was probably Eilersen, grabbing his elbow to steady herself.

'Stand still,' her grandfather advised her. 'The effects will wear off in a few more seconds.'

That turned out to be optimistic, but Joy was relieved to find that her vision did indeed gradually return to normal. She was even happier to see, as her grandfather swam into focus, that his eyes were both confused and worried . . . and most definitely blue.

'What was that?' Eilersen asked, pulling off his glasses and squinting.

'A harmless but effective line of defence against intruders,' said Grandpa Blake. 'Harmless to *most* types of intruders, anyway. Who are you?'

'I'm Daniel Eilersen. I'm a . . . schoolmate of Justin's.' He didn't bother stretching the truth as far as 'friend'.

Her grandfather sighed quietly to himself. 'Justin. Yes, of course, he would be right at the centre of things. I'd hoped . . .' He didn't finish, but turned to look at Joy. 'Perhaps you'd better tell me exactly what's gone on here.'

Still slightly dazed, not to mention weak-kneed with relief, Joy was grateful when he led the way into the living room and motioned for them both to take seats. She fiddled with the silver necklace, its continued coolness reassuring, as she tried to figure out what to say.

'What made you come home early, Grandpa?' she asked. 'I know you called Dad on Friday—'

'I have an . . . alarm, of sorts, placed on my study,' he told her. 'It's designed to let me know when someone is in there without my permission. Admittedly, I've never tested it from as far away as America before – but as it turned out, it worked admirably.'

Joy couldn't help but cringe. 'Then you've always known when me and Justin were in there?' All those childhood years of slipping into forbidden territory for a quick peek, quite convinced of their own impressive sneakiness.

'Of course.' His eyebrows lowered, but the annoyance was not directed at her. 'And of course, I knew that with bright and curious children like yourselves, it was inevitable. Forbidden fruit is twice as tempting as any other kind; if I'd had my way, you would have been taught the dangers of magical knowledge long ago, instead of being kept away from it entirely.'

'But Dad didn't want you to teach us,' Joy said, still weighed down by her guilt. They might not have known that the book was so dangerous, but they'd certainly known that going behind their grandpa's back to borrow it wasn't right. There was no way to blame *that* on their father's attempts at censorship.

'No. No, he certainly did not.' Grandpa Blake sighed, looking his age for once as his usual vibrancy slipped away. 'And maybe it was foolish of me, but I wanted to see my grandchildren grow up, so I abided by his wishes.'

'Dad was going to cut us off from you if you tried to tell us anything?' Joy was appalled, if not totally surprised.

'Your father is almost wholly irrational when it comes to matters of the occult, my dear,' her grandfather said regretfully. 'I did what I could to protect you, but he's done his best to stamp out even those enchantments that can only be used for good.'

Joy's grip tightened automatically around the necklace. Could it have warned her of the danger in time if her father hadn't hidden it? Or would Justin have talked her into going ahead with the ritual anyway? She had a nasty feeling that he might have.

'So you suspected that your family might be in magical danger?' Eilersen asked.

Grandpa Blake frowned slightly at the blunt enquiry. 'It was too much to hope that they never would be,' he said coolly. 'The trouble with magic is that its consequences are always greater than they seem, and a single ill-advised decision can come back to haunt you many years later. On the surface, the occult is an easy answer, and easy answers tend to come with hidden costs attached.'

'Buy now, pay later,' Eilersen muttered to himself.

'Exactly.' Grandpa Blake looked across at Joy. 'I knew that Justin had found the grimoire – the book – some time ago, but I foolishly hoped he would accept your father's insistence it was all make-believe and never do more than look at it. I should have known better; items of power have ways of exerting influence over the unprepared, and that one in particular is far more than just a book.'

His face grew stonier, and Joy shuddered inwardly. 'That does *not* mean, however, that I hold either of you free from responsibility for your actions,' he added starkly. 'I think you had better tell me exactly what damage you've done – and then we can figure out what, if anything, we can do to set it right again.'

Joy swallowed hard. Until that moment it hadn't truly occurred to her that Grandpa might *not* be able to help them.

'We, um – it was Justin's idea,' she began, then winced at the way that sounded. 'Not that I'm trying to . . . I'm just saying, it was Justin who started it all. He had the book with him on Friday when he came home.'

'He had it at school,' Eilersen supplied. 'I noticed because he had his nose stuck in it all lesson. That's not like Justin, even if he's not looking at schoolwork. He doesn't usually have that much of an attention span. And the moment I got near him, he started daring me to come and see him do magic. He was just looking for an excuse.'

'Why'd you go along with it?' Joy asked. For somebody who claimed to be a lone wolf, he seemed to have been manipulated into taking part just as easily as the rest of them.

Eilersen frowned. 'Because it was . . . strange. Justin is' – only a brief wry smile suggested he'd paused to consider who he was talking to – 'basically shallow. He's not into mysticism, and he's definitely not into anything that would make him look uncool. So I couldn't see why he was wrapped up in such a flaky idea. I assumed it was some kind of set-up to make me look like an idiot.'

'And being basically a know-it-all, you had to go along just to prove you could see through it,' Joy concluded.

Eilersen gave her a very small smile. 'Something like that.'

'I think I can guess how things went from there,' Grandpa Blake interjected, gently herding them back in the direction of the subject. 'And you, Joy, were also persuaded to take part . . . Was there anyone else?'

'Trevor Somerville,' Joy supplied.

'Four of you. I should have known.' He sighed to himself, aware of the significance of the number. 'So what happened?'

'We summoned a spirit,' Eilersen said baldly, not even trying to justify it.

Grandpa Blake let out a great, angry exhalation of breath that Joy was sure would have been a swear-word had it not been for her presence. 'Of course. Too much to hope that he would have begun with any lesser ritual. The spirit managed to escape, naturally?'

'It wasn't Justin's fault,' Joy blurted, feeling like somebody should be sticking up for him. 'He tried to do the banishment as soon as things started going wrong, but Dracherion was already out of the circle.'

Her grandfather's reaction to the name was elec-tric. His eyes opened wide, and he half stood up out of his chair. 'The spirit identified itself as Dracherion?' he demanded urgently.

'Justin couldn't command it to give up its real name,' Eilersen said.

Grandpa Blake straightened up the rest of the way, his face still paper white. 'No,' he said softly. 'A spirit's true name is the one thing you cannot instruct it to reveal – and the one thing you most need if you are to have a hope of dealing with it safely. This is one particular case where I desperately wish I knew it myself.'

Joy searched his expression worriedly. 'You've met Dracherion before, haven't you?' The strength of his reaction had scared the hell out of her.

'I have. And if this means what I think it does, then the situation is far, far worse than I imagined.' He strode towards the doorway, then paused to look back at them. 'Come with me, both of you. Time is short, and there are answers we need to look for.'

XVIII

Grandpa Blake returned to his study and pulled things out of the corner cupboard until he came up with a wooden chest. He opened it on the desk and tugged out the cloth lining. There was nothing else inside.

He stared into the empty box for a moment and then sighed. 'I'm an old fool,' he said, half to himself. 'I should have changed the seal on this box the moment I knew Justin had found it, but I was too afraid of damaging the existing enchantments. Assuming they even remain.' He locked the box again and then motioned to Eilersen. 'Open it.'

Eilersen frowned, but stepped forward and tried to turn the key in the lock. He couldn't budge it. 'It won't.'

Grandpa Blake nodded to himself. 'Joy?'

Joy expected the key to be stiff if it moved at all, and almost wrenched her good wrist when it turned without the slightest effort. 'Only our family can open it?' she guessed, lifting the lid.

Her grandpa nodded again. 'A blood seal. Simple, but secure.' He looked pained. 'Or perhaps it would have been, had I been able to warn you and your brother not to breach it. I tried to obey your father's wishes, but I should have known better. Ignorance is never a protection.'

He hauled open the desk drawer and began going through it as he spoke.

'My own first brush with the occult came when I was at university. I was part of a group of enthusiasts – dreamers, mostly, with no real idea what we were doing. Our rituals never really amounted to much, and most of our members soon drifted away in search of better thrills. But it was through that group that I met Anthony Fullman.'

Eilersen shot Joy an enquiring glance, but she didn't recognize the name. 'Who was he, Grandpa?' she asked.

'A young man with big dreams – dangerously big. For him, the occult was not an idle hobby, but a raging obsession.' He paused as he produced a jar of something waxy from the drawer. He sniffed its contents carefully, then began using his fingertips to rub it over the inside of the chest.

'At the time, of course, I didn't see it that way. He was driven, and it was easy to believe he was destined for greatness. He neglected his studies, got thrown out of his lodgings and wasted so much money he could barely afford food . . . and yet, somehow, he could always convince me that everything was well in hand, and the big breakthrough was coming any day.'

'And then he found it,' Eilersen said.

Grandpa Blake nodded soberly. 'Somehow – I never knew the details, and I doubt I would want to – he managed to get his hands on a number of rare and very dangerous books. You've seen one of them for yourselves; trust me when I say that several of the others were far nastier. I disposed of those after he died. I only wish it had been possible to do the same with this one.'

'Why couldn't you?' Joy asked.

Grandpa Blake held up a hand for silence. 'Hold on a moment, please.' He screwed the lid back on the wax and picked up a tin full of grey powder. He tipped some out into the palm of his left hand and drew patterns in the dust with his little finger, muttering quietly in a language that she didn't understand.

When he was done, he raised the hand to his face and blew the powder out over the chest. Instead of scattering everywhere, it collected, like iron filings drawn to a hidden magnet. Joy and Eilersen crowded in to see as a pattern of lines emerged on the base and sides of the chest.

'Is that good?' Joy asked uncertainly.

'It's not, is it?' Eilersen's sharp eyes had spotted the faults in the pattern. The design looked like it should have been symmetrical, but several lines towards the centre were broken or bowed outwards.

Grandpa Blake closed the box, gaze distant. 'It's bad,' he confirmed. 'Extremely bad.' He turned away from them and went over to stand at the window. He was silent for a long time.

'I had hoped when you told me the spirit called itself Dracherion,' he said finally, 'that some lesser spirit had simply adopted the name. They do that at times – try to borrow a more intimidating reputation – and the real Dracherion, or so I prayed, was still safely sealed away.'

'In the chest?' Eilersen said.

'In the book,' her grandfather corrected, and Joy gasped. 'Handling the book, or even casting spells from it,' he was quick to tell her, 'should still have been perfectly safe. It has a binding spell placed upon it, which is rather like a trap for magical energy. Spirits can move in and out of objects even more easily than they can living beings, but if the object in question has a binding on it, they find themselves stuck and can't get out again. They can't do any-thing to remove the spell while they're inside it, so they're effectively sealed up until a human being comes along and undoes the binding.'

'We didn't do that,' Joy said, shaking her head nervously.

He sighed. 'I know. It appears Dracherion is even cleverer than I gave it credit for.' He rubbed his face, looking tired. 'I knew there was a small trickle of energy escaping through the binding. There always is, especially when you trap such a powerful spirit. But it seemed to me it would take Dracherion a thousand years to escape that way. I put the seals on the chest to keep a check on it, and left it at that.'

He shook his head at himself. 'I should have realized that the spirit had a plan. It couldn't do much with so little energy, but it could do enough: attract Justin's attention, help him to spot the right spell, subtly prod him into wanting to perform it. The pull of the summoning ritual was so strong that it overrode even the binding, and Dracherion was able to leave the trap to answer it. If we could force the spirit back into the book, it would become trapped again . . . but it won't be easy to catch it the same way twice.'

There was silence for a moment. Joy shifted uncomfortably. 'So, um . . . how did Dracherion get into the book? Was it a spirit you and Anthony summoned at university?'

Her grandfather shook his head. 'No. No . . . and perhaps that's unfortunate. If we'd brushed up against such great danger back then, we might have thought twice about continuing. At the time, however, we were convinced that our magic could solve anything – even the problems it had actually created.'

'Like gambling to try and fix your gambling debts,' said Eilersen.

'Exactly that. And with far higher stakes than just money or possessions: we put our lives, souls and everything else on the line in ways that it's taken a lifetime to even try and patch. My continued studies of magic are as much self-defence as an inability to kick the habit. The spirit world is not to be looked into lightly and then forgotten about.'

Joy shuddered. 'But you woke up eventually,' she said, as much to reassure herself as prod the story onwards.

'I met your grandmother,' he said simply. 'It made me look at my life through an outsider's eyes, and I didn't much like what I saw. Anthony was a madman, and I'd been blindly following him down a terrible path. I knew I had to cut all ties with him before it was too late.' He looked solemn. 'Even so, if it hadn't been for the opportunity my graduation gave me to make a clean break, I'm not sure I would have succeeded.'

'Where does Dracherion come in?' Eilersen asked.

'Some time after.' Grandpa Blake looked distant. 'I began a new life with Mary and tried to channel my thirst for magic into less harmful areas: writing, studying, collecting. I made a particular effort to learn all I could about magical charms and protections; I knew by then that Anthony and I had left ourselves open to terrible danger, and I had my wife and children to think of.'

'Children?' Joy blurted, startled. Her father was an only child – her only aunts and uncles were on her mother's side. 'But I thought—'

Her grandfather raised a hand to forestall further questions and continued. 'Your father's birth was rather a difficult one, and it left your grandmother ill and weak for a long time afterwards. I wondered then – and sometimes still do – if there were dark influences at work, but the fact is that medicine then was not what it is now, and it could just as easily have been the kind of plain, ordinary misfortune that haunts any family. We were relieved that your father proved to be a strong and healthy boy, but further children seemed unlikely – until, almost a dozen years later, we had Lilian.'

'Lilian,' Joy breathed, and felt nervousness clutch her insides like a cramp in her gut. This would answer so many questions, and yet suddenly she wasn't sure she wanted to hear it. An aunt of whom she'd never heard, whose name her father wouldn't even speak . . .

Her grandfather's face, already grave, had gone very still and controlled. It was a long time before he spoke again.

'Lilian was . . . not as fortunate as her brother,' he said, too evenly. 'Mary had an even worse time during her second pregnancy, and afterwards was plunged into a deep depression that she never really recovered from. Lilian was born prematurely, and her babyhood was plagued by illnesses: she had a weak heart, frequent trouble with her lungs . . . Yet for all that, she was a remarkably happy child.'

He gave a small, wistful smile that Joy found painful to look at. She glanced sidelong at Eilersen and saw that he was looking down at his hands, bony fingers linked together in front of him.

She waited for an awkward while, then interrupted her grandfather's reminiscences with a respectful cough. 'Then, um . . . then what happened?' Her voice came out rough and scratchy.

'Very little,' said Grandpa Blake softly. 'Lilian's troubles only grew worse as she grew older, and there seemed to be nothing anyone could do to stop it. We tried every remedy the doctors could suggest, and a few more they would have laughed off as ridiculous . . . Eventually Mary was even willing to let me try those healing magics that my studies could suggest. But nothing worked. Our little girl was dying before our eyes.'

Joy gave him a sad, sympathetic smile. 'So you went back to the black magic.'

He let out a slow, heavy breath. 'I contacted Anthony. I knew full well it was a terrible idea, but I had none better, and the thought of sitting back and doing nothing . . . Well, if going down that path again had been the end of me, at the time it seemed a small enough price to pay.'

Grandpa Blake paced over to the doorway – an excuse to look away, perhaps, more than simply restlessness.

'Anthony was only too eager to help. I'm tempted to say it was a chance to show off his powers that drew him, but that's probably unfair. I'm sure he honestly believed that his spells would solve everything. He was too blind to their faults to think anything else.'

Eilersen interrupted the building silence. 'Was it his idea to summon a spirit?'

Joy saw her grandfather's shoulders slump, although he still stood with his back to them. 'Oddly enough, it was mine. His books held darker, more direct ways of restoring a person to health, but I didn't want Lilian subjected to them. I thought that if we called upon a spirit to help us, then we would be able to banish it afterwards with no lasting harm done.'

Joy could think of nothing to say, and gazed miserably at the ground. Her grandfather had summoned Dracherion in an act of terrible desperation. Why had *they* done it? For fun? To see if they could?

Why the *hell* hadn't she stopped Justin?

'Did you and Anthony do the ritual alone?' Eilersen asked.

Joy didn't quite get the question, but her grandfather whirled round, as if reacting to some implied accusation. Then he relaxed a little, looking resigned.

'You're no fool, are you, boy?' he said, smiling bleakly. 'Yes, you're right. It took four of you this time, and it took four of us then. Anthony would have volunteered some friends of his to help out, but I thought even having him involved was a big enough mistake. So, to my shame, I felt obliged to ask Mary' – he shot an inscrutable look at Joy – 'and your father.'

'*Dad?*' she blurted, starting in shock.

'Yes. He was seventeen at the time, and I had misgivings about involving him, but there was no one else. We performed the ritual, calling upon a spirit that Anthony had summoned up many times before. I don't know whether he decided to call it by the name of Dracherion, or if that was something the spirit itself chose to adopt. Either way, it was clear that the spirit was much stronger than any we had summoned in our younger days. Unfortunately

Anthony was just the type to taunt a being of great power because he had a temporary advantage over it.'

'How did Dracherion get loose?' Joy asked him. She remembered with a shudder how they'd childishly delighted in the snow that had caused their downfall.

'All too easily.' Her grandfather grimaced. 'It was a mistake, a terrible mistake, to involve your father and grandmother. It recognized their inexperience and nervousness, and preyed upon them. Before we knew it, it had escaped . . . and taken possession of Anthony. His reckless activities had left him wide open to magical influence, and the spirit was able to take over his mind completely in a matter of moments.'

'But you managed to get it out again,' Joy said, leaning forward in desperate hope.

'In . . . a sense,' he said softly. 'I couldn't perform a proper exorcism to send Dracherion back to the spirit world. The ritual had given it links to the four of us – if I cast it out of Anthony, it would have been free to come straight back and attack one of the others. So I did the only thing I could think of.

I placed the binding spell on the book and forced Dracherion to jump into there. I couldn't hurt it or banish it, but I could keep it trapped.' He looked shrunken and defeated. 'Or so I thought.'

'But it worked in the short term,' Joy said eagerly. If Dracherion took possession of one of them, they would be able to get the spirit out again.

'Yes . . . and no.' Grandpa Blake blunted her optimism with a slow shake of his head. 'Anthony . . . was left wide open by his dangerous addiction, without any mental defences. The possession completely destroyed his mind. Eventually I forced the spirit to leave, but what it left behind was nothing but a shell.'

'He died,' Joy said numbly.

His eyes, when they met hers, were bleak. 'He died,' he confirmed. 'And Lilian followed, days later. It was the final straw for poor Mary. She ended up taking her own life in remorse – and your father has never forgiven me for any of it. Perhaps he was right not to. If I'd known my old sins would come back to haunt my grandchildren, I would never have tried to involve myself in your lives.'

He sighed softly. 'I'm afraid, Joy, that the solution to this may be beyond even my expertise. I will do all I can to save all of you . . . but I can't promise I will succeed.'

J ustin struggled out of sleep with an effort. Trevor was shaking him by the shoulder, and it took a while to remember where he was and why he had slept on the floor.

He groaned and pulled away from the touch. 'Jesus, Trevor, leave off. It's the middle of the— day,' he finished lamely, as the blinding sunlight penetrated. He squinted at his watch in disbelief. How could it be almost noon? He didn't feel like he'd slept for ten minutes.

'Here. Drink this. It'll wake you up.'

A steaming mug of coffee was thrust into his hands,

and Justin reluctantly pushed himself up into a sitting position. He took a quick gulp and made a face at the bitter taste.

'Aw, man.' Normally he didn't mind coffee, but today even the smell was making him nauseous. He set the mug aside after only one more sip and struggled to focus on Trevor. 'OK, OK, I'm up. What's going on?'

'We have to get to your granddad's,' Trevor said, sounding agitated. 'Joy called me. She and Eilersen are already there. I think they've been trying to fix everything without us.'

Justin grimaced, unwelcome recollections of the night before filtering in. 'Yeah, well, maybe they should be.' He gingerly picked up the book from where it had fallen when he dozed off. As he turned it over, he saw that Dracherion's symbol was no longer visible on the covers. 'It's gone,' he observed, running his fingers over the leather.

'Maybe that means whatever Dracherion tried didn't work,' Trevor offered tentatively.

'Maybe,' Justin said dubiously. Or maybe it just meant the spirit was covering its tracks. He wasn't sure the book would be any use to them, but the idea of leaving it behind – or worse, trying to destroy it – made him shudder uncomfortably.

Was that his reaction he felt, or the spirit's? It was a disturbing question.

'Did Joy say if she and Eilersen had found anything?' he asked nervously.

Trevor shook his head. 'She just said to meet them both over there.'

'OK, then.' He had to accept a hand up from Trevor to pull himself off the floor. 'Guess we'd better get going.'

That turned out to be easier said than done. Justin was so tired he could barely *move*; he felt as if he'd been running a marathon in his sleep.

His mind was fuzzy from exhaustion as he walked – or maybe it was from something else. Was Dracherion still in his head even now? He could imagine its influence spreading like a fungus, eating away at every trace of what made him Justin Blake. How long before he lost himself completely?

Maybe Joy had found some way to stop it. His

heart quickened with hope. Why else would she and Eilersen summon them to Grandpa's house? They had to have come up with something.

Or maybe they hadn't. Maybe Trevor had told them that he was already possessed, and they'd decided there was no way to save him. Maybe this was a trap, and he was being led to his death.

OK, that was just a crazy thought. Joy was his sister. She'd never go along with that.

Unless somebody – like, oh, maybe *Eilersen* – had convinced her that it was the only way. That sacrificing him was their only hope of stopping Dracherion. Would she agree to it then?

Justin didn't know if he should hope that she would, or hope that she wouldn't.

By the time they reached his grandfather's house, he'd obsessed over the possibilities so much he was sure he'd be ready for anything.

Until Grandpa Blake answered the door.

'Justin. I think perhaps you'd better come in,' was all he said.

The shock was enough to clear Justin's head a little as he followed him into the house. His grandpa was dressed not unlike the image Dracherion had projected, but he could tell instantly that this was the real thing. His face was a stern mask, but Justin could sense the hurt and disappointment lurking beneath it. Emotions that the fake version hadn't displayed, because in order to feel them you had to *care* about the person who'd angered you.

Justin would almost have preferred to face Dracherion.

'Grandpa!' he blurted, struggling to keep up with his grandfather's long strides. 'What are you doing back?' As dazed and confused as he was, he was still sure it wasn't Monday yet.

'I was alerted the moment you entered my study,' his grandfather said, and Justin cringed inwardly. 'I got here as soon as I could . . . but it seems it wasn't nearly soon enough. Your sister has told me everything.'

Not quite, Justin thought – because unless Trevor had spilled the beans, she didn't *know* everything. She didn't know it was him Dracherion had chosen to possess. He took a deep breath. 'Er, Grandpa, there's something I should tell you—'

Trevor gave a strangled squeak. Justin broke off

to glance at him and saw that he was urgently shaking his head. No? No what? He *shouldn't* tell his grandfather about the possession? But surely . . .

Grandpa Blake urged him onwards impatiently. 'I'm sure you have all sorts of justifications for your actions, but I really don't have time to stop and hear them. We have a lot of preparation to do before the ceremony can start.'

'Ceremony?' Justin followed him through to the next room and found the long wooden dining table covered with books and papers. Joy and Eilersen were seated at one end, heads together over a diagram. Justin felt a wave of distrust wash over him at the sight. Those two, together – *again*. And what was it with Joy phoning Trevor's house this morning, instead of calling Justin's mobile directly? And why hadn't anyone warned him that Grandpa Blake had come back? Were they *all* sneaking around behind his back?

They had good reason to, he reminded himself, but the thought still stung. Who was to say, just because Dracherion had possessed him once or maybe twice, that all the others were totally safe? Any one of them might be equally compromised.

He regarded Eilersen with cold suspicion. Maybe he'd been premature in assuming that Dracherion had been using him all along. After all, there was still no proving what had happened in the early hours of Saturday morning. The spirit might have only hijacked his body last night because its usual vessel wasn't around.

'Oh . . . hey, Justin,' Joy said distractedly. Eilersen didn't acknowledge his arrival at all. While he kept his head bowed down over the book, whatever expression was on his face stayed well hidden.

'From what Joy has told me, Dracherion is very close to its full strength already,' Grandpa Blake warned. 'This house has certain protections that allow us to plan in safety, but we must return to the site of the original summoning to complete the ritual. All traces of the spirit's presence must be purged at the same time: from the site, from the book and from the four of you.'

That hit way closer to home than Justin liked, and he pulled an exaggeratedly unhappy face to hide it. 'OK, now, when I think purging, I think vomiting, and—'

'The greater the hold the spirit has over you, the more unpleasant the experience will be,' his grandfather said starkly. 'But it has to be done, and it has to be done *now*. If Dracherion is allowed to take total possession of one of your bodies, then rooting it out becomes far more difficult and dangerous.'

Justin swallowed and exchanged a glance with Trevor. With the level of control Dracherion had already shown, could complete possession be that far behind? Grandpa Blake needed to know just how close it would be.

And yet Trevor was still giving him the 'please, *please* don't tell him' signals.

What? he mouthed forcefully, but all he got in response was a pleading stare. And then Eilersen was watching them suspiciously, so he had to wait a while before he could drag Trevor off to the kitchen and demand some answers.

'Justin, you *can't* tell your granddad that Dracherion's been possessing you,' Trevor blurted as soon as they were out of earshot.

'Why not?' he demanded, utterly at sea. After what Grandpa Blake had said about the extra danger, it seemed that warning the others was more important than ever.

'Because it's not—' Trevor shook his head, babbling in his agitation. 'You mustn't— You just *can't*. If your granddad thinks that *you're* the one who— He'll do it all wrong!'

Justin scowled at him, unable to dig through the stammered words for any coherent explanation. 'Do *what* wrong?'

'Justin, I . . .' There was a long, tortured pause. 'Y-you're his grandson,' Trevor said finally. 'And if it's, um, if it's harder on you the bigger Dracherion's influence is, then—'

'Then he might not be willing to do what he has to,' Justin completed sourly and ran a hand through his hair. Maybe Trevor had a point. His grandpa already knew Dracherion planned to take one of their bodies, and surely he knew better than any of them how soon the spirit could manage it. Letting him know for sure that the target was Justin might only make him nervous about what had to be done.

And he couldn't help but think of Eilersen's suspicious behaviour. What if Dracherion had been working on *both* of them? Maybe his control of Justin had been just a bluff to keep them all looking the wrong way.

'OK,' he said, and Trevor almost collapsed in relief. 'You're right. I'll keep my mouth shut for now. But that means I'm relying on you to watch me. If it looks like *anything* might be happening, you've *got* to let the others know right away.'

'I will,' Trevor said, nodding frantically. But Justin couldn't help but wonder if they'd made the right decision.

If they didn't warn Grandpa what to expect, then he wouldn't have time to get anxious about the idea of hurting Justin, or be caught out if Eilersen was the real target. But he also wouldn't know that Dracherion had managed a second act of possession since Saturday morning.

If their silence led Grandpa Blake to underestimate the spirit's strength, they could be headed for total disaster.

The planning session stretched on for hours. Justin could barely sit still or concentrate on the words he was being drilled on, conscious of every second trickling away. He hadn't eaten, but his stomach was too unsettled to risk putting food in it. All this calculating and rehearsing only underscored how ill-prepared they'd been before.

It was growing dark when Grandpa finally sighed and sat up in his chair.

'I could do with another dozen years to train you,' he said soberly, 'but this will have to do. Dracherion's magic will only grow stronger as the night progresses.

Given the choice, no doubt it would wait to make its move until the early hours – but make no mistake, it will be almost at full strength already. We have to go now.'

They headed out into the wintry afternoon.

'What if somebody sees us?' Joy said uneasily as they left their grandpa's driveway. It was drizzling faintly, but not yet quite dark, and it wasn't particularly late.

'I doubt very much that they will.' Grandpa Blake shook his head as he adjusted the strap of his leather shoulder bag. 'Dracherion is much stronger than when it first broke free, but appearing to too many people at once would drain its energy. Dark magic leaves invisible but highly unpleasant traces; it won't be difficult for the spirit to drive people away.'

'It gives them the creeps,' Eilersen surmised.

'Gives *me* the creeps,' Joy muttered, hugging her cardboard box close against her. They were all carrying bags and boxes of things Grandpa needed. Justin patted the bag at his hip, making sure that the book was still there.

A car passed, and once or twice a pedestrian, but

no one looked twice at their little procession, even loaded up as they were. Perhaps Dracherion's dark influence was working already – or perhaps they just didn't look half as suspicious as they thought they did. It was surreal to think that nobody else was the slightest bit aware of the deadly final showdown that was brewing.

Justin fell back to walk beside Trevor, still feeling a little too wobbly to keep the pace that his grandpa was setting. An alarming spread of blurry lights was encroaching on the edges of his vision.

'How're you feeling now?' Trevor asked, peering at him intently.

'I'll be fine,' he said curtly. He didn't want to dent Trevor's confidence. If the ritual banishment relied on their strength of will, the last thing they needed was for him to start spreading his doubts around.

'You just seemed a bit . . . shaky.'

'Yeah, well, it's sodding freezing,' Justin countered sharply. But he was beginning to worry that he really would be sick; nausea was rising, and he couldn't tell if it was thanks to the motion of walking, butterflies in the stomach, or something far more serious.

'I'm sure you'll be OK to play your part,' said Trevor, and gave him a brief smile. Justin grimaced back and kept walking.

'This is the place?' asked Grandpa Blake when they reached the entrance to the park.

'Yeah.' Joy rattled the handlebars of her bike, still chained with Justin's to the fence. Justin looked at the ruined tyres and wondered if it had been him who'd crept over here and slashed them. It seemed ridiculously petty, but maybe Dracherion had made him do it as an afterthought, just for kicks. Enjoying the fact that he was sabotaging himself without knowing it.

The rain had dried up, but the sky was overcast, and the whole park was shrouded in darkness. Or at least, it should have been. Justin assumed for a moment that his eyes were playing tricks again, but no: there was a faint blue glow shining up from the ground ahead.

'Ah.' Grandpa Blake looked pleased. 'The circle of protection may have been breached, but it looks like its power isn't gone completely.'

'Which is good, right?' Joy prodded optimistically.

'It gives us hope, at least. Without a body to use

as a permanent anchor, Dracherion must keep using the weak point created by your ritual to access our world. If we seal it, as should have been done at the end of the summoning, the spirit won't be able to return on its own.'

'I'm guessing we have to throw it out first before we can lock the door behind it,' Eilersen said pessimistically.

Grandpa Blake sighed. 'Unfortunately, yes . . . and that's going to be the difficult part. Everyone, move in close around the circle. We have to establish a new perimeter around it.'

'With us on the inside,' Justin said grimly.

'Everything the spirit may have tainted must be contained.' His grandfather nodded. Trevor looked dismayed, but personally, Justin was relieved. He didn't want to be the one weak link that caused the plan to fail.

'But, Grandpa, you weren't involved in any of this,' Joy protested. 'Surely you could stay outside the circle and you'd be safe?' The guilt of dragging him into their self-made nightmare was obviously weighing on her.

Grandpa Blake stood firm. 'Saf*er*, perhaps,' he corrected, 'but my expertise will be needed, and I am in many ways responsible for this whole mess. And even if I were not, I would not have my grandchildren fight such a terrible battle alone.'

'Then at least take this.' Joy lifted her hair and pulled off the silver necklace to hand to him. 'You're the only one who understands all the rituals. There's no point in me being protected if Dracherion manages to get at you.'

He recognized the sense of the gesture and accepted it graciously. He slipped the necklace around his own neck and then straightened up. Justin was aware of looking at him from the outside for perhaps the first time; seeing a tall, imposing, dignified man instead of just crazy old Grandpa.

'The ground for the ritual must be prepared,' Grandpa Blake said. 'Stay close together, for after the circle is formed, no one can leave until this is over. If the protective circle is broken before we finish, we'll lose our only chance of banishing the spirit before it takes over a body.'

From what he'd told them, the odds of things

ending well after Dracherion completed the possession were a whole lot slimmer. It wouldn't just have
to be cast out from its stolen body, but also prevented
from jumping straight into another one. That meant
either trapping it, or forcing it back into the spirit
world entirely – neither of which would be easy. The
spirit would fight tooth and nail to prevent it, and
the host body would bear the brunt of the damage.

And Justin was slated to be the host body. He swallowed hard.

At Grandpa Blake's direction, Joy walked around
them in a wide circle, pouring out a ring of salt. The
closing of the loop felt more final than it should have
done, as if they were sealed in by something much
harder to cross than a line of salt a few centimetres
wide.

'These designs must be copied out exactly. The
tiniest deviation could be disastrous.' Grandpa
handed the sheet of paper across to Eilersen: Justin
assumed he'd been bragging about doing the artwork
the last time round. He didn't challenge it. He didn't
trust his own hands not to shake, and Trevor was
staring blankly into space. Joy was chewing on the

ends of her hair, a mannerism he thought she'd given up in junior school.

Justin ended up doing little to help with the preparations. His head was still swimming, and once the incense was lit it grew even worse. The air was too still: no wind to interfere or snuff out candles, but also none to disperse the cloying scent of burning herbs and oils. Chalk dust and pepper hung in the air, making his eyes sting and his throat prickle.

Trevor was in charge of setting out the candles, and he was beginning to look almost as sick as Justin felt; more than once he was sharply corrected by Grandpa Blake for putting something in the wrong place. Once lit, the candles surrounded them with a bright ring of flame, making it nearly impossible to see outside the circle. Justin hadn't quite anticipated the heat; it was the same sort of uneven toasting you got from a bonfire, some parts uncomfortably close to the flame, others still utterly frozen.

Eilersen finished his painstaking chalking, and then Grandpa Blake added more symbols. 'Be sure you're seated in the same order as you were during the summoning,' he said. 'Justin, I'll be on your left.

Everybody kneel down facing inwards, and whatever you do, do *not* disturb any of the chalk.'

Justin would have needed no prompting to be very, *very* careful on that count. He winced as he settled his aching body into position, thinking that he'd be lucky if he could stand once this was over. Assuming there was any *him* left to do the standing.

With the ring of candles blocked out by their kneeling bodies, the centre of the circle was extremely dark. The burning incense in the centre produced no light, only thick, dark smoke.

'For the first part of the ritual, you must echo my words,' Grandpa Blake directed. 'Remember how we rehearsed it earlier.'

He lowered his head and closed his eyes for a moment, meditating or just taking a second to calm himself. Justin tried to do the same, but relaxation was a lost cause. His fears and worries circled endlessly, and the relentless throb of his headache made the dark behind his eyelids swim and shift.

Would Dracherion even answer their call? Were they only fooling themselves that they could banish it before it completed the possession? Grandpa Blake was sure they had a chance – but he didn't know what Justin knew. He didn't know how close they were really cutting it.

'We will begin.'

Justin opened his eyes in time to see his grand-father straighten up and raise both hands, palms out flat in a defensive gesture. 'By these candles I call upon the force of fire, to cleanse the evil from this place in scouring flame,' he intoned. His voice, always commanding, now boomed out over the park.

'By these candles we call upon the force of fire,' they echoed raggedly, 'to cleanse the evil from this place in scouring flame.'

'By the fragrance and the smoke I call upon the force of air, that the darkness here be driven away to where it can harm none.'

The group echo that time was crisper and clearer, four voices turned into one as they spoke together.

'By the salt of the sea I call upon the force of water, to wash away the taint of evil in purifying waves.'

'By the salt of the sea we call upon the force of water, to wash away the taint of evil in purifying waves.' Justin could almost hear the waves, and the logical voice that said it was probably blood rushing in his ears was the one that seemed out of place right now.

'By the ground beneath I call upon the force of earth, to banish instability and heal the rift that should never have been opened.'

As they repeated the words, Justin could feel the ground beneath him thrumming, or maybe it was the air, or maybe it was everything at once. Energy was building, flowing through the five of them like electricity through a circuit.

The lines of their previous magic circle glowed; not with blue light this time, but a dull red like the rings of a hob warming up. Justin could see the ugly gash in the design where Dracherion had broken the circle. Heat radiated out from the pattern, and the virulent smell of hot tarmac mingled with the stink of incense. He fought the urge to gag.

Grandpa Blake raised the book from his lap and thrust it forcefully into the middle of the glowing design. The pages immediately burst into flames. Justin gasped and made an automatic grab to rescue it.

His grandfather hauled him back. 'Do *not* cross the boundary line!' he reminded them.

Justin stared with his heart in his mouth as the spellbook was consumed by fire. And then he realized that it wasn't actually *burning*. Flames licked around it, but the pages didn't curl or blacken.

He suddenly remembered, with a chill, the vision shown to them by the magic mirror. Hands on the spellbook, dark energy being sealed in . . .

What had Dracherion done to the book when it marked the covers? Had it found a way to prevent whatever his grandpa had done before from working a second time?

'Grandpa—' he blurted, determined to spill all, but his grandfather motioned for him to be silent.

'There's no more time to talk,' he warned. He grabbed hold of Justin's hand. 'From now on, we must be very careful. Link hands, and don't let go before I tell you. The slightest misstep here could be fatal.'

Justin could only hold his tongue, and pray they hadn't made that step already.

It felt like Justin's shoulders were being wrenched out of their sockets. His grandfather's crushing grip anchored him on one side, Trevor's sweaty hand on the other, and in the middle he was tense as a stretched elastic band. He felt like he'd go flying forward into the circle if they suddenly let go.

'Spirit Dracherion, you have outstayed your welcome,' Grandpa Blake boomed. 'This world will no longer tolerate your presence. Reveal yourself, and prepare to be banished!'

Justin's own hands tightened convulsively, and his

teeth ground together hard enough to make his jaw ache.

Nothing was happening.

'Reveal yourself!' Grandpa Blake commanded again.

Blistering heat bathed Justin from all sides and he was sure he was beginning to hallucinate; spots appeared before his eyes, and the shadows flickered. Clouds were hurtling across the sky, and the smoke and candle flames all danced.

And still Dracherion didn't appear.

'Why isn't it *working*?' Trevor demanded, in a high, nervous voice. He made as if to pull his hand free, but Justin held on tightly, and he could tell from his sister's grimace that she was doing the same. They couldn't afford to let a moment of panic ruin everything.

'Reveal yourself, or prepare to be revealed!' his grandfather bellowed in his ear, and Justin flinched.

Come on, come on, come on, he was silently praying with gritted teeth, but still there was no response. Dracherion was not going to answer their summons.

And yet Grandpa Blake looked more resigned than disturbed. He sat back and sighed, and the tension that had built up in the circle gradually bled away.

'I suspected that the spirit wouldn't make this easy for us.' He released Justin's hand and spoke in a more normal tone of voice. 'It's fighting the summons. We're going to have to use the magical links it has to the four of you to call it to us. I need you all to take hold of the book.'

'Do *what*?' Joy yelped, staring at him in dismay.

Eilersen regarded the blaze warily, and Trevor went pale.

'But . . .' He looked to Justin for backup, but Justin couldn't give it to him. He knew they had no choice but to trust his grandfather's directions – no matter how dangerous they sounded. He steeled himself, and before he could think twice, leaned forward and reached into the flames.

His left hand immediately felt like it was on fire, and he panicked and drew back partway. Then he realized that the pain wasn't even coming from the licking flames, but from the knife-slash across his palm. The fire didn't burn, just washed around his hands like warm water; not quite real, not completely an illusion.

He took a deep breath and bent forward, grasping the blazing book with both hands.

It was agony. He might as well have poured acid directly into the wound. Justin's eyes streamed, but he bit down on his lip and refused to let go. He wasn't going to be the one who doomed everybody else.

Joy haltingly followed his lead, relaxing when the flames didn't harm her. Eilersen studied them both for a moment, then leaned in and joined them.

Justin waited for Trevor . . . and waited, and waited, and finally nudged him in the side. Trevor swallowed miserably, but sat forward. When he closed his fingers around the leather binding, Justin felt the same surge of power as before. The sensation of a circuit being completed.

'The spirit is bound to you by the hairs and the blood you contributed to its summoning,' said Grandpa Blake, at his shoulder. 'It will be bound into the book by a spell I worked long ago. You must invoke it and command it to appear as you did before.'

Justin's eyes went wide. If Dracherion had done something to the book, then the binding spell might not work properly. But Eilersen had followed the prompt before there was time to call a halt. 'I evoke and conjure thee, Spirit Dracherion, by the element of air, and by my own mind.'

Across from him Joy cleared her throat. 'I evoke and conjure thee, Spirit Dracherion, by the element of fire, and by my own heart,' she said soberly.

'I evoke and conjure thee, Spirit Dracherion, by the element of water, and by my own will,' Trevor said in a small voice.

And then it was Justin's turn, and the words of the invocation he'd used once before took an age to dredge up from his memory. Grandpa Blake had made them rehearse the enchantments again and again, but it had all blurred together in his head. What was it – what was it . . . ?

'I evoke and conjure thee, Spirit Dracherion, by the element of earth, and by my own hand!' Justin gasped out. The first ceremony, when he had so blithely sliced open his palm and begun this, seemed more than a lifetime ago.

'Quickly, Justin, the rest of the invocation!' His grandfather thrust a sheet of paper into his lap, which was just as well, for his head was pounding too fiercely to recall what he'd been drilled on. It took everything he had just to force the angular handwriting into focus.

'Return, Spirit Dracherion, and show the— *thyself* within the circle. By the . . . ties . . . of sacrifice we call thee. By the – um, by the instrument of thy binding we command thee. By the words of power we have mastered thee.' His speech became less faltering as energy welled up within him, and his vision grew brighter and clearer. 'Do thou come forthwith, and cause neither harm nor havoc, but make answer to our enquiries, and seek not to deceive or to bargain. Appear before us now, in guise neither fearsome nor objectionable, and do not vanish or by subterfuge appear to vanish until we grant thee thy discharge. So I command thee!'

'So we command thee,' the others chorused after him.

The clouds raced, and everything seemed preternaturally bright as adrenaline fuelled Justin's night vision. A gust of wind set the smoke in the circle to billowing.

No, wait. Not wind.

The dark smoke spun in a way no air currents could have achieved, and then the flames around the book flared outwards. Justin threw his hands up in defence as they surged towards his face. A blast of heat washed over him, and blinding light turned the insides of his eyelids red. He let out a choking gasp of pain.

When he could see again, Dracherion was in the circle.

The spirit wore a new form now, vaguely human in shape but composed of liquid fire. The dead eyes were like holes drilled through the sheet of flame, looking onto somewhere dark and terrible. In his dizziness, Justin felt like he was falling forward into them, drowning in an absolute vacuum.

He wrenched his gaze away desperately and felt a selfish stab of relief as he saw that the others had also let go of the book, when he knew he should have wished that they'd held firm. Dracherion stood unopposed in the centre of their circle, and they had all shrunk back from it. If their weakness gave the spirit power, they were handing it over right now.

But for the moment, it seemed, the spirit had eyes for something more interesting than the four of them. A malevolent smile curved briefly through the shimmering flames.

'Lucien Blake,' it acknowledged smugly. 'You think to command me with such an embarrassing charade? Have you fallen so far in your dotage, or do you hope to bargain for your life by bringing me these pathetic infants?'

'They are stronger than you know,' Grandpa Blake said calmly, 'and none of us will bow before you. This world is not for your kind; leave peaceably now, or be expelled.'

Dracherion laughed, a sound like the crunch and crackle of burning wood. 'You have no more power than you did thirty years ago, old one, and even less strength of will. These children have at least provided me with a vessel for use in this world – you are too old and feeble even for that.'

'No one here is going to be your vessel,' Grandpa Blake said coldly. 'Link hands!' he directed the four of them again, prompting another amused chuckle.

'Yes, why not? Sing your holy songs and make your

little gestures. These toys cannot vanquish me – they are mine to command!' Dracherion threw out an arm, and the candle flames that surrounded them suddenly stretched and shot upwards, trapping them all in a cage of fiery bars.

'Stay focused,' Grandpa Blake warned them tightly. 'It's trickery – the spirit is trapped inside the circle and hopes to make us forget that fact. Ignore everything it says and focus on the banishment.'

Dracherion shifted forms again and took on the shape of a little girl that Justin recognized from the photos. 'Yes, of course, listen to the old man. After all, his decisions always turn out so *well*,' she said, in a voice far more cruel than any child that age could come by naturally.

Justin swallowed hard and avoided looking at his grandfather. Joy had filled him in on the tragic fate of their Aunt Lilian. The grip on his cut left hand tightened enough to make him gasp with pain, but when his grandpa spoke again his voice was level.

'The banishment,' he repeated, carefully controlled. 'Justin, repeat the words as I tell them to you. I hereby license thee to depart, Spirit—'.

'I hereby license thee to depart, Spirit,' he echoed, straining to pick up his grandfather's murmured words through the snapping, crackling buzz of a head-splitting sensory overload. 'And go in peace, to the . . . what? To the realm from whence thou came . . . Seek not to return here, until – until such time as I call upon thee again, and harm none in departing. I compel thee to obedience by the laws that . . . by the laws that govern thy kind, and by the power that binds thee—'

Dracherion threw back its head and *laughed*, the shape of the little girl grotesquely melting and elongating, developing coiled ram's horns and huge bat wings that blotted out the sky. 'You dare to try and trap me here by the power of your pathetic binding spell,' it bellowed, 'but *I am not bound!*'

The magic flames licking around the spellbook seemed to freeze solid – and then the whole thing just shattered into pieces, fragments flying outwards. Their circle of joined hands fell apart as they tried to shield their faces from missiles that burned like acid. Justin heard Eilersen cry out in pain. Joy was patting madly at her hair, as if trying to put out a fire.

His grandfather had gone as white as milk. 'The book—'

'Can no longer act as any prison to me.' Dracherion chuckled, and the ground shook. 'Fool, Blake, did you think your handiwork so sacred I could do nothing to touch it? That because only human hands could lift the spell, I would have no way to remove it? Where I cannot go, there will always be those who can act for me – and the weak-minded are such easy prey. My servant, come to me!'

Justin felt an agonizing wrench to his insides, as if his guts were being drawn out of his body. He screamed and fell forward, knowing he was dying, knowing there was no way he could possibly stand pain like this for a single second longer . . .

And knowing, in a rush of understanding that came just as consciousness drained out, that he'd been wrong.

Dracherion wasn't trying to force its way into his body. It was sucking his own life energy out.

He wasn't the one it was calling for.

Justin howled like he was being murdered, a horrifying raw sound of unrelenting agony. Joy screamed as he pitched forward, convinced that he was dead – or worse. As Dracherion vanished from the circle, she forgot her grandpa's every warning and ran across it to get to her brother.

His eyes were still open, but they were glassy, and his lips were beginning to turn blue. His skin was so pale it might have seemed bloodless – if it hadn't been for the evidence of it seeping from the cut on his palm. His whole left hand was an angry, puffy red, as if ravaged by some terrible infection.

He was breathing, but only very shallowly, and Joy's hands shook too much to take a pulse. She struggled to remember her first aid, determined to keep his vital signs going by brute force if they wouldn't continue alone. But then hands were dragging her away from her brother's body, and she lashed out blindly.

'Let me *go*!' She was only vaguely aware of shouting as she struggled with someone taller and stronger. '*Justin!*'

'Joy, look out!' a voice yelled next to her ear, but it didn't mean anything until a knife slashed down out of the darkness, millimetres away from biting into her arm.

She whirled round and saw Trevor coming at her a second time. He was holding her grandfather's ceremonial knife in a frighteningly natural grip, and his face was completely dead. There was no recognition in his eyes; no hesitation, and certainly no mercy.

She might have stood staring until she was killed if Eilersen hadn't pulled her away.

'Trevor's the vessel!' he shouted. There was barely any distance between them, but things were moving so fast and so confusingly that quiet words probably wouldn't have reached her. 'I thought it was after Justin, but it must just have been drawing on his energy! He offered it blood – it can get more power from him than it can from the rest of us.'

Joy's eyes flickered back to her brother's slumped form. He'd been pale and tired, but she'd thought it was just shock and fear. Dracherion must have been drawing energy from him all the time. And now that the spirit had taken a body, all moderation had been thrown out. It didn't need him kept alive as a power source any longer – it could just keep on draining until he was completely dry.

'How do we *stop* it? Grandpa?'

She cast around for her grandpa and saw that she'd been only a target of opportunity; Trevor, or who-ever he was right now, was going after her grand-father.

He sure as hell didn't *move* like Trevor. Her brother's friend was big, but he was podgy rather than solid, and he usually crept around trying not to draw attention to himself. The stranger that wore his face now used the same body like the bulk of a prowling tiger, every movement filled with purpose and restrained might.

Her grandfather was backing away, and Joy was aware all over again of just how old he was. He was a very fit man, but it was crazy to think he could wrestle with a strong and healthy teenager – let alone one under magical control.

'Come on!' she ordered Eilersen. It wrenched her heart to leave Justin, but she knew that without Grandpa Blake they had no chance of helping him.

Joy charged across the grass after Trevor. There was no hope of doing it stealthily, but he seemed so oblivious to all but his task that she prayed they might have a chance. With no time to dream up a sensible plan, she simply launched herself at him in her best flying tackle.

It was like diving head first into concrete. Trevor was heavy for her to bring down in any case; under Dracherion's control he was steady as a rooted tree. She struck him with enough force to bruise her whole body, and he didn't even stumble or rock backwards.

'For God's sake, Trevor, if you're in there, fight this thing!' she shouted, clinging on. He knocked her away with a brutal backhand, and then spun to kick out at her shin.

For a deceptive instant the impact barely hurt. Then the hot tingle flared into unbearable torture; her eyes filled with tears and she could barely gasp enough breath in to swear. She sank to the ground. Trevor raised the knife.

'Joy, give me some help here!' Eilersen came barrelling out of the darkness to grab Trevor's upraised arm, trying to wrench it round behind him but barely even able to move it. 'Get his other arm!'

The idea of just getting off the ground seemed like too much to ask, but she threw herself forward with a whimper. She could hardly support her own weight, so she let it all hang from Trevor, doing her best to hamper him all she could.

It was like trying to grapple with an angry squid. Trevor was so strong they could barely hold him between them, and ridiculously, inhumanly fast. He kicked, bit and tore, and every time she thought she had a handle on him, he seemed to develop a few extra joints. He smacked them both around as if they were rag dolls.

Eilersen gasped and doubled over from the force of a shoulder driven into his stomach. Joy saw her chance as Trevor was momentarily bent over, and raised her hands to crack him over the head. He caught her wrists before she could even finish the swing, shoving her backwards. Another kick to her bruised leg and she was flat on her back on the grass, rolling away just in time as the knife slashed down close to her face.

Then her cheek stung, and she realized that he hadn't missed at all.

'Joy!'

She looked up at her grandfather's shout, and saw something flash through the air towards her. It was too distant to catch, and as she stretched over to grab it from where it lay on the grass, Trevor hauled on her foot to pull her backwards. 'Eilersen!' she wheezed.

'I'm kind of . . . busy . . . at the moment,' he gasped out, hanging onto Trevor's knife arm for dear life.

Joy pulled up her free foot and used it to try and prise the shoe off the other one.

Finally the battered trainer popped off, and she scrambled forward on her hands and knees, scarcely able to breathe.

She patted wildly at the grass in the darkness, and her fingers brushed the silver chain of her necklace. There was no way she would get a chance to put it on, so she wound the chain around her fist as she rolled over.

Trevor was coming at her, grinning like a maniac, and Eilersen was too far back to help, clutching his nose and his bent pair of glasses in his hands. Joy raised the pendant instinctively, thinking of nothing more intelligent than to shove it in his face for a second of distraction.

Trevor faltered, and she thought for a moment that she saw a flicker of his terrified grey eyes behind Dracherion's empty black. Then he snarled and lashed out at her arm with the knife.

The swing was wild – maybe that momentary battle for control had thrown off Dracherion's aim, or perhaps she was just lucky. Either way, she didn't wait around for it to happen twice, but threw herself forward, holding the chain out in both hands as if to choke him.

She got it around his neck, and it was heating up in her hands – burning hot, like a metal saucepan

on the stove. Her fingers were blistering, but she
didn't dare let up. Trevor's struggles were fading now,
concentrating on getting the burning chain away
from his skin instead of fighting her, and she was
able to force him backwards.

'Get him against the fence!'

Suddenly Eilersen and her grandfather were both
with her, helping wrestle the raging Trevor towards
the edge of the park. Joy slammed him up against
the chain-link fencing with no finesse, unable to spare
a thought for the innocent boy who might still be in
there with Dracherion. She could see through the
fence to the street beyond, and it was massively surreal – the whole world had narrowed down to this
life-and-death struggle, until it seemed that normal
things like cars and houses couldn't belong in it.

They had Trevor pinned against the fence, but
there was no chance of relaxing their guard at all.
He was still hissing, kicking and trying to bite, snarling
curses and filthy threats in what sounded like dozens
of languages.

'What do we do now?' Eilersen blurted. He'd
shoved his glasses in a pocket or just dropped them;

his face looked young and underdressed without them. His usual air of calm and competency was shattered by his ragged breathing and dishevelled appearance.

She was no better off herself. There was blood dripping down her face and she had no way of telling how deep the gash was. She didn't dare lift a hand from Trevor to reach up and feel it.

'Our only chance now is to try and perform an exorcism,' her grandfather panted. 'I can do it, but I need my hands free, and the two of you won't be able to hold him alone.'

Joy glanced over her shoulder, but her brother's unconscious form was lost in the shadows, and the sudden head-butt that smashed into her jaw had her hastily facing forward again. 'We can't afford to wait until Justin wakes up!' she protested. They had Trevor trapped right now, but they couldn't keep it up for ever; already her overstretched arms were tiring.

'While Dracherion's using him as an energy source, Justin probably *won't* wake up,' Eilersen reminded them. 'So again I say: what do we do *now*?'

Joy looked to her grandfather for answers, but he

was breathing heavily, head hanging down. She was suddenly caught by the selfish terror that he would have a heart attack right there and then, and leave the two of them stuck here, trying to hold Trevor by themselves.

Bright light shone in her eyes. She twisted her head away, thinking it was some trick of Dracherion's, and then she realized it was coming from beyond the fence. Headlights. Headlights on the road outside.

She expected them to swish straight past without stopping, but instead the car screeched to a halt, and that was worse. Her heart leaped into her throat as she saw the driver's door fly open and realized what their current position must look like. If some have-a-go hero came running and tried to haul them off Trevor . . .

'Grandpa—'

'Just hold on,' her grandfather ordered, his voice ragged. 'Whatever happens, you *must* hold on.'

But her numb grip was slipping, her injuries were screaming, and Joy knew she couldn't keep it up much longer.

The car door slammed, and a tall figure came running towards them. It wasn't until a streetlight picked up a flash of greying red hair that Joy realized it was her dad.

'Thomas!' Her grandfather threw out a hand towards him. 'Come here! We need your help.'

Her father charged through the gates at speed, but he slowed to a halt as he recognized them all and registered their position. 'What the hell is going on here?' he demanded furiously.

Trevor took advantage of the opportunity to play innocent. 'Mr Blake,' he said pleadingly, voice high and tremulous as if the guttural snarls had never been. 'They're all crazy. Please—'

'*Don't* listen to him,' Eilersen warned urgently.

'There's dark magic at work, Tom – don't let the boy fool you,' Grandpa Blake snapped.

The horrified look on her father's face was more complicated than simple shock. 'You *promised* me, Dad!' he said, voice broken by hurt and disappointment. 'You promised me you would never get my children involved in this. Where's Justin? Joy, get away from him.'

'We got *ourselves* involved, Dad,' she cut in quickly, struggling to keep her grip on Trevor's jacket. He had gone completely limp, but she knew it was just a ruse – if they let up, they could be dead in seconds. He didn't have the knife in either of his trapped hands, but had it been dropped, or was it just tucked away somewhere? They couldn't risk letting go for long enough to find out.

'I came home as soon as I realized something was wrong,' Grandpa Blake insisted. 'I gave my word I wouldn't teach them magic, and I kept it. Justin found one of my books—'

'There's an evil spirit on the loose, it's currently in Trevor, Justin's not going to wake up until we get it out – we'd appreciate some help,' Eilersen rapped out succinctly.

'It's not true!' Trevor babbled, sounding desperate. 'They're all nuts, he's brainwashed them – please, Mr Blake, you've got to help me—'

'God, *shut up*!' Joy rattled him against the fence in frustration. She didn't want to think her dad could be fooled by such a blatant ploy, but he still wasn't moving. She could see the indecision playing out across his face: he didn't *want* to believe them, that was the problem. He'd rather buy into his own lie that Grandpa Blake was a crazy old man than accept there was magical danger.

'Dad, you *know* it's got to be true,' she pleaded with him. 'Dracherion's back, and Justin will die if we don't do something to stop it!' If her brother was even still alive.

'The exorcism is our only chance, to save this boy and Justin,' her grandfather said earnestly. 'Get my bag, Thomas! It's somewhere down there on the grass. Now, before it's too late.'

Her father hesitated for a moment longer, then finally he moved to go for the bag. Trevor let out a howl of rage and slammed himself back into Joy. She cried out, almost knocked off her feet, as Eilersen and her grandfather wrestled to keep him in place.

'Justin!' Their father had spotted Justin's prone form, and immediately abandoned his mission to go over to him. 'I'm not sure he's breathing!' he shouted a moment later, and Joy lost her grip on Trevor entirely.

'He may still live!' Grandpa Blake insisted, throwing himself on top of Trevor as he made a lightning-fast attempt to dart away. 'The spirit has been drawing on his life-force – banish it from this world, and— Aah!' A punch to the jaw sent him reeling, and then Trevor was getting away.

'Dad!' Joy yelled, sensing it all about to spin out of control. Eilersen was on his knees; she yanked him up, not bothering to stop and see what injury had put him there. They both staggered along after Trevor.

Unfortunately Trevor's objective was not to escape. He turned on them, smiling as if this was the most

274

fun he could possibly imagine. The wicked knife-blade glinted in his hand.

'Why didn't you take that thing *off* him?' she shouted at Eilersen in disbelief.

'I thought you had!' he retorted, equally incredulous. They dived to either side as Trevor came lunging towards them, and damn it, he was coming after her again.

The necklace – of course, she had the necklace. She could drive him back with that . . .

She'd *had* the necklace. Joy realized she'd dropped it at some stage, and she didn't have the slightest clue where. She couldn't take her eyes off Trevor long enough to search the grass.

'Trevor, come on,' she begged him. 'You must be in there – you must be able to fight this. Come on, Trevor, you don't want to kill me . . .'

She only just managed to roll to the side as he did his level best to prove her wrong. He hauled her up by her collar, and she squeaked out a startled swearword. She kicked, but she couldn't break his grip – there was *no way* she was going to get out of this alive . . .

Until salvation rose up behind him.

Something must have shown in her eyes, because he pulled back and started to wheel round, but not in time to avoid the crashing blow to the side of the head her father dealt him.

Even that didn't take him down – he hit the ground, but was fighting to get up again immediately. Her father didn't give him a chance, pinning him down with a knee to the centre of his chest.

'Joy! Daniel! Get his arms, get them trapped underneath him!'

Somehow Joy found the strength to get up again, and grab and twist Trevor's flailing hand until he finally let go of the knife. She snatched it up and hurled it overarm across the playground, not caring where it landed as long as it was as far away as possible.

Only with her father's full body weight holding him down and both arms trapped behind his back did Trevor finally go limp. He seemed docile and defeated, but none of them were crazy enough to relax their grip for a moment.

'Tom, we're going to need your assistance,'

Grandpa Blake panted, hurrying over to join them. 'I believe I can safely cast the spirit out of the boy, but there's no way the children can hold him by themselves.'

Her father's face froze up completely. He said nothing, but Grandpa Blake obviously read his increase in tension.

'This is *not* the same situation as thirty years ago,' he said forcefully. 'Anthony was corrupted long before Dracherion took hold of him; he was too steeped in dark magic to be freed of it. This boy is much less tainted – we can save him, if you help us!'

'He lies,' said the hoarse, alien voice of the spirit, no longer even pretending to be Trevor. 'Your father will kill the boy to save his own skin, and Justin will die with him. These children mean nothing to me; my business is with the old man. Let me go, let me deal with him as I wish, and the boys will go unharmed.'

Eilersen let out a snort of total disbelief, but Joy could see the words striking home with her father.

'Dad, its *business* is to hurt as many people as it possibly can,' she said desperately. 'You can't listen to it.'

'Oh, of course, yes, trust the old man's word.' The dark self-satisfaction on Trevor's usually mild face was quite obscene to look at. 'It's so much more reliable. After all, he's never broken a promise, has he? Never sworn to save the life of someone and then failed to deliver . . . If you seek to shake me from this body, Justin *will* die.'

'You said, before, that you couldn't *do* a direct exorcism,' Joy's father said accusingly. 'That if you tried, the spirit could just jump straight into one of the other summoners.'

'I'm stronger now,' Grandpa Blake said seriously, not a boast but a statement of fact. 'There's a much better chance—'

'Not good enough, Dad!' he shouted. 'No *chances*. You fight magic with magic, and it *always* goes wrong. What if it jumps into Joy? I'm not losing both of my children to your madness.'

'You may not lose either, if you *do what I say*!' her grandfather thundered.

'Of course, that's right, prove your point by shouting the loudest!' her father yelled back.

Grandpa Blake's face went cold. 'This is no time

for adolescent temper tantrums,' he said warningly.

'Oh, because that's what any argument against you has to be! Well, you're wrong, Dad, because I don't need to be swayed by evil spirits and I don't need to be an idiot teenager not to listen to you. I'm not listening to you because *I don't trust you.*' The anger abruptly fled, leaving behind dismay and misery. 'You can promise me any outcome you like – but you promised me before, and you were wrong. So what am I supposed to believe?'

Her grandfather was silent for a long moment and then looked him solidly in the eye. 'You're supposed to believe that whatever I promised and didn't deliver, I did my best to give you, but it didn't work,' he said simply. 'I tried . . . and it just didn't work. And if I thought there was a way to resolve this without further risk to the children, if I truly believed I could give my life for Justin's, I would do it in a heartbeat . . . but I don't.'

The silence lingered, until Trevor took advantage of it and tried to throw them off. Joy swore violently and fought to hold on. 'Dad!' she yelped urgently, as Eilersen took a blow to the stomach.

'Make a decision,' Grandpa Blake ordered, reaching for his bag. 'You're going to be right, or you're going to be wrong, but this is the only chance you're ever going to have, so *make a decision*. Will you help us or not?'

'I swore I would never, ever get involved in your magic again,' her father grunted, helping to hold Trevor's thrashing legs.

'We all make promises,' her grandpa said, without any hint of smugness.

Her father closed his eyes in surrender. 'Do what you have to do.'

It seemed as if a whole lifetime had gone by in the space of minutes. Joy felt like they'd been arguing for hours, and yet she still hadn't had enough time to stop and catch her breath.

Trevor didn't seem to suffer from any such problem. If anything, his struggles had grown even stronger. Without her father's added weight and strength they never could have held him.

It wasn't exactly a picnic *with* him. Not only was the spirit's stolen body stronger and faster than any human had a right to be, but he seemed able to go completely boneless, like a cat shrinking away from an unwanted touch. Throwing all their combined weight on top of him was the only way to gain any control at all.

'Before we cast Dracherion out, we must first seal it into the host body,' Grandpa Blake said, kneeling on the grass as he quickly unloaded items from his leather bag. 'If I try to exorcize the spirit while it still has links to the rest of you, it will simply escape through one of them. It will be difficult and painful to sever the connections, but the only way to force it back into the spirit world is to leave it with nowhere else to go.'

He began to smear some kind of paste or oil over Trevor's cheeks and forehead, leaving thick streaks that glistened in the candlelight. The herbal smell was strong enough to make Joy gag, but Trevor's reaction was even more violent. He gave an inhuman shriek of rage and pain, and his whole body rippled as if he was trying to bring his guts up.

'Oh, God, he's going to puke,' she groaned, unable to imagine having to deal with that on top of everything else.

'Puke *that* way,' Eilersen said sharply, turning

Trevor's head to the side as her grandfather sat back on his heels.

'Be wary of trickery!' he warned.

'I am! I'm also wary of vomit!'

They all flinched as Trevor was racked by a series of dry heaves, going on and on until he was sobbing and choking. When they were finally over, he collapsed, limp, against the ground. Hating that she had to do it, but knowing they could afford no mercy, Joy helped the others keep his shoulders pressed to the ground.

Grandpa Blake unceremoniously yanked Trevor's shirt open and began giving his chest the same treatment as his face, painting arcane symbols with the oils. That seemed to wake the spirit up, and Trevor started struggling again, swearing and snarling. Joy couldn't help but shudder when the baleful glare focused on her. There was no hint of anything behind it but pure, unadulterated hatred.

'Tom, get his shoes and socks off,' her grandfather ordered as Trevor hissed and tried to arch away from his touch. 'I'll need to anoint his palms and soles – quickly, while he's still relatively weak.'

Relatively. As her father shifted position, Trevor took advantage of it to kick him in the face. There was another round of yelling and squirming, until Eilersen succeeded in driving a knee into his belly to hold him down. The spirit cursed and spat obscenities. Joy wasn't sure whether Dracherion could feel the pain, and it certainly didn't seem to care about it. How were you supposed to deal with an enemy that was just as happy to hurt its own hijacked body as to damage anyone else?

Her father wrestled Trevor's trainers off, face deathly grim. Her grandfather was murmuring words as he painted shapes on Trevor's skin, ignoring the way he shied from the touch as if it burned. Occasional syllables reached her, but she couldn't tell if the chant was in English or some other language entirely.

Trevor groaned, a low, deep sound of suffering. His skin was waxy grey and by now drenched with sweat, disgustingly clammy to the touch.

'Dad, this is obscene,' her father objected, aghast. It was hard to remember, even seeing the dark flare in Trevor's eyes, that it was the spirit their actions were torturing, not her brother's long-time friend. And really, *should* they remember that? Somewhere, down below the surface, Trevor was still in there too.

'It's Dracherion's presence that's hurting him,' Grandpa Blake insisted forcefully. 'Its energy is toxic to him, but we *have* to seal it all in before we can get rid of it. If we don't purge all its influence at once, it will pop up again, like a cancer.'

He took a deep breath and produced a glass orb from his bag, cupping it in both hands. He moved his lips in the rhythm of an inaudible chant, and the orb started to glow with a blue light that lit up the bones in his fingers like an X-ray. 'Joy, Daniel, brace yourselves,' he warned urgently. 'I'm about to sever the connections.'

Before Joy could ask exactly what they should be bracing for, the light flared.

The world went pure white, and there was suddenly an incredible *pull* deep inside her, like a hand trying to yank her intestines out. She gasped and gagged as if she was trying to vomit up something huge, like a parasite that had been growing in her gut until it was bigger than anything she could have swallowed. Her mouth filled with the coppery taste of blood.

Beside her, Eilersen was retching, folded over on the grass with his arms wrapped around his belly. And Trevor . . .

Trevor was *screaming*, but she couldn't hear any sound. His face was contorted, and he was thrashing too violently for her father and grandfather to hope to hold. She knew she should help them, but her whole body was shaking, her hands gouging holes in the dirt as every muscle tensed up against that *something* that pulled and pulled and pulled—

And finally snapped.

Joy collapsed, and the world swam around her. Her eyes stung with tears – not just from pain, but from a feeling of loss so strong it was almost like grief. Something had left her. Something foul and evil that should never have been there – but at the same time, something so *huge* that she couldn't help but be rocked by its departure.

She lay staring dazed at the sky, until with a flash of fear she remembered Justin. If he'd just gone through a disconnection even stronger than she had . . . Joy scrambled to her feet.

She spotted his unconscious form a few metres away and ran over to him. His skin was cold; not just clammy like Trevor's, but as cool as the grass he was lying on. And . . . 'Dad! He's not breathing!'

'Your foolish ritual has cut the cord that was keeping him alive,' Dracherion rasped in a voice that barely resembled Trevor's any more. The spirit's stolen body was obviously greatly weakened; he could hardly lift his head off the ground. 'If you want him to live, release me!'

'You wouldn't help him, even if you could,' Grandpa Blake said icily. 'Joy, come back here!' he called. 'We must hold the banishment *now*, before Dracherion regains its strength.'

'But—' They couldn't just *leave* Justin. If they started CPR— If Grandpa did some kind of spell— If they just *pretended* to take Dracherion up on its offer—

'*Now*, or all of this has been pointless!' her grand-father ordered.

'Joy.' Her father's voice was quiet and thick with

grief, but it moved her where Grandpa Blake's bellow couldn't. 'Do as he says.'

Her limbs as heavy as if they'd been dipped in lead, she rejoined her father and Eilersen. They had Trevor laid out on his back; feeling like she was watching her actions from somewhere far away, Joy helped them pin his arms out wide from his body. Trevor's muscles jerked and spasmed, as if he was going through some kind of slow-motion seizure, but he still found the co-ordination to raise his head and fix empty eyes on her.

'And so your brother *dies*,' Dracherion said, with venomous triumph. She flinched, but didn't let go.

Her grandfather knelt down beside her. 'Spirit, your presence will be tolerated in this vessel no more!' he intoned. 'Depart now, or face the consequences!'

Trevor's mouth opened to spit some curse or taunt, but Grandpa Blake moved with rattlesnake speed to grab him by the jaw. Through some sleight of hand he produced a glass vial and tipped its contents straight down Trevor's throat. The boy spluttered and gargled, flecks of foam spotting his lips.

'He'll choke . . .' Joy's father warned anxiously.

She had a hand clamped on one of Trevor's shoulders, Eilersen was restraining the other, and he was left with no way of righting himself to spit the liquid out or clear his airway.

'Dracherion won't let him,' her grandfather said with confidence. 'It can't leave Trevor's body. If it lets him die, it's as good as banished.'

'Well, no, that's not *quite* as good!' Eilersen said tensely. 'Can you get it out *without* killing him?'

Grandpa Blake took a deep breath. 'I intend to try. Joy, your necklace—'

'I don't have it!' she blurted, dismayed.

'It's here.' Eilersen handed it across to her, and she fumbled and almost dropped it again.

'Place it against his chest, over his heart.'

She did, and cringed back as Trevor began to howl, a horrifying unearthly sound of suffering. Her father shifted uncomfortably. 'Dad, this is—'

'*Necessary,*' her grandfather said brutally. 'And don't assume, because he seems so pitiful, that the tricks are over yet. Hold him still; I must get Justin.'

Joy tried not to look at Trevor's face as they continued to hold him down. He was shuddering, sweaty and pale, and now with his eyes fallen shut he looked all too human. She couldn't make herself believe that it was only the spirit in pain; she could see the skin of his chest reddening where the heat of the pendant was blistering and burning.

Forgive us, she found herself muttering inside her head. *We're doing everything we can. Please forgive us.*

Her sympathy for Trevor was driven from her as her grandfather approached, her brother's still form cradled in his arms. It seemed to her that her grandpa should never be able to carry him; he shouldn't be so light or seem so fragile.

'Dad?' her father said uncertainly.

'Justin's blood began this,' Grandpa Blake said grimly. 'We'll need him here to end this.' He laid Justin down beside Trevor with extreme gentleness.

Joy couldn't take her eyes off her brother. How could he possibly be so still? Her brother was *always* constantly in motion – even in sleep he thrashed and snored and muttered. This couldn't be the real Justin; it was just a shell.

A body.

She didn't dare ask the question, and her father

didn't speak. It was Eilersen who tentatively broke the silence. 'Is he . . . ?'

'I don't know,' Grandpa Blake said bleakly. 'We won't know, one way or the other, until this is over with. Now, join hands with me. We must try to work the banishment again.'

They formed a circle around the boys. It was impossible to step back far; even with her arms extended as far as they could reach, Joy was close enough to have trodden on them. Trevor looked as bad as Justin now, his body juddering uncontrollably, and his skin turned a colour approaching charcoal. Joy couldn't help but fear that even if this worked, neither one of them would live long enough to know about it.

'I hereby license thee to depart, Spirit, and go in peace to the realm from whence thou came,' her grandfather began in a sombre tone. 'Seek not to return here until I call upon thee again, and harm none in departing. I compel thee to obedience by the laws that govern thy kind; I compel thee by the power of the pendant that constrains thee; I compel thee by the will of those who gather to oppose thee. Thy vessel is lost to thee, thy power is removed, and the bonds that anchor thee to this world are failing. Depart, and return to trouble us no more.'

He nodded towards the other three, and after a moment of hesitation, they came together to repeat the words.

'Depart, and return to trouble us no more.'

There was none of the hot, electric energy Joy had felt screaming through her veins during the summoning. Instead, there was something else here: a quiet, sober sense of important things shifting somewhere just beyond the visible. Power – but a slow, stately sort of power, like the forces that kept the world turning.

It was the other side of the coin, she recognized. The kind of magic that brought Dracherion into this world was like the incredible burst of man-made energy needed to fire a rocket into space; this was like the entirely natural pull of gravity to bring it back down.

There was no puff of smoke, no light display and no thunderclap to signify Dracherion's departure, but she felt it all the same. The sense of things slotting back into their natural positions, like the resumption of a sound that she hadn't realized she was missing.

She dropped Eilersen and her father's hands at the same time as they let go of hers. It was over.

Dracherion was gone. But what about Justin and Trevor?

'I t's Trevor!' Justin blurted as he sat bolt upright, coming out of the haze.

Sitting up so fast made him light-headed. He felt strangely *clear*, like his ears had popped – as if some great pressure had suddenly lifted, and things that had been blocked out were flooding back in.

He realized he'd been lying on the grass in the park. It was night, but the clouds overhead had cleared, so that now a little moonlight peeped through. He could see Eilersen sitting cross-legged a short distance away, watching him.

'It's Trevor,' Justin managed to croak out again,

295

though he suspected that the warning wasn't worth much now. Whatever had happened here was obviously long over.

'We figured that out a while ago,' Eilersen said dryly. 'But thanks for playing.' He was trying to give a disdainful sneer, but it kept curling up at the corners.

Eilersen was a mess. His normally immaculate hair was sticking up in all directions, and he seemed to have lost his glasses. There was a dark smudge of dirt or blood on the side of his chin, and the collar of his jacket was torn.

Justin sat back and assessed his own state. He was still aching all over, but it was the clean, simple ache of having pushed his muscles too hard – nothing at all like the horrible feeling he'd been battling for days. His headache had gone, and so had the pain in his left hand. When he brought the palm up close to his face, he saw only a narrow, pale scar that could easily have been there for years.

'Justin!' He was almost knocked to the ground as his little sister tackled him from behind. 'You're awake!'

'Well, I *was*, until you jumped on me,' he groaned,

struggling to sit up again. 'Wow, what happened to you?' he asked as he got a good look at Joy's face. There was a jagged cut down her right cheek as if someone had slashed her.

'Trevor,' she said simply.

'Oh.' Justin was about to say more when a heavy hand landed on his shoulder. He started to look up. 'Hey, Grandpa, did you—?' But the concerned face that loomed over him did not belong to his grandfather. '*Dad?*' he said in disbelief.

He was pulled up off the ground and into the biggest bear hug he'd had since he was about six years old. 'If you *ever* do something this stupid again, you're getting grounded until you're seventy-five,' his father grumbled into his shoulder.

'OK,' he agreed mildly. If he did anything this stupid ever again, just getting out of it *alive* would be more than he had any right to hope for. He was lucky enough to have managed it this time.

Justin couldn't imagine what his father was doing here, but it seemed easiest to just lean against him for support without trying to ask. He looked around for his grandpa and spotted him crouched down a short distance away. He seemed to be leaning over something laid out on the grass—

Oh.

Justin left his father's side and staggered over to where Trevor lay slumped. His grandfather looked up as he approached and gave him a small relieved smile.

'Justin. How are you feeling?'

'Better,' he said simply. 'What about Trevor? Is he all right?'

He hadn't figured out that Trevor was the one who was truly possessed until moments before he'd lost consciousness. As Dracherion had stepped up its attempts to drain him dry, he'd finally recognized the tug that he'd been feeling all along. The spirit hadn't been trying to force its way in – it had been drawing power *out*. He hadn't blacked out those times because he was possessed, but because Dracherion was burning up a bigger amount of his energy.

Energy that it needed to possess somebody *else*.

And if that was true, there was one very obvious suspect. Because Trevor had to have been lying about what had happened when they'd broken the magic mirror.

Grandpa Blake frowned down at the unconscious boy. 'He survived the exorcism, but it's been a great shock to his system,' he said. 'I hope that the possession was brief enough to have done him no permanent damage physically, but as to the other effects . . .' He shook his head grimly.

Justin was silent. It had been bad just to spend a day *thinking* Dracherion had possessed him. If Trevor had been aware of what was happening, seen and felt everything the spirit did but been powerless to stop it . . .

'Still, we should all count ourselves very lucky indeed,' his grandpa said heavily. 'Trevor could have died – and you probably should have. A bond sealed in blood with a spirit that strong is not something to be broken lightly. Your sister and Eilersen only suffered some unpleasantness when I cut the connections, but I honestly didn't know if you would survive.'

'So, um . . . why *did* I survive?' he asked awkwardly. 'Just pure luck?'

'Pure spite on Dracherion's part, as it happens.' His grandfather smiled tightly, but his eyes were cold. 'I think what must have happened is that it stopped your heart just before I severed its connection to you. Not to give itself any sort of useful advantage, you understand – purely to make sure that our victory was as hollow as possible. But as it turned out, that malicious parting gesture was the very thing that saved you.'

'My heart stopped?' Justin said incredulously. He placed a hand over his chest, half fancying he could feel a weakness to the beat.

Grandpa Blake nodded soberly. 'You were, in many senses, effectively dead – and so the bond between you and the spirit broke more easily. If your body hadn't been in the process of shutting down at the time, you would probably have lost your mind, if not your life.' He seemed outwardly calm, but the tiny tremor to his hands betrayed how much he was shaken. 'When we completed the banishment, your heart started to beat again. Still, if it had taken us only a few minutes longer . . .' He trailed off, unwilling to voice the possibilities.

'I'm all right now, Grandpa,' Justin reminded him softly.

'I hope so.' He sighed. 'But I fear tonight's events

will leave their mark on you, one way or another. Magical wounds never heal cleanly, and you may well have lost years off your lifespan.'

Justin took that news without much reaction. It was hard to think about consequences so far in the future when he was still trying to catch up with tonight. 'Yeah. Well, I suppose . . .' He paused as he noticed that Trevor was stirring, and bent down to give him a cautious nudge. 'Trev?'

There was a brief pause, then Trevor's eyes opened as tiny slits. 'I hate you,' he said hoarsely.

'Yeah, yeah.' Justin smiled and offered him a hand, but Trevor pushed it away roughly and sat up.

'I *hate* you,' he repeated petulantly, and Justin took a startled step backwards at the degree of venom in his voice. Trevor's eyes were now their usual grey, but his normally meek and nervous face was contorted with a fury Justin had never seen before.

'You don't even *know*, do you?' Trevor burst out as he climbed unsteadily to his feet. 'You never notice *anything*. If it's not about you, then it's not important. *I'm* not important. I'm just supposed to be your little charity project who follows you around and does whatever you tell me. Did you even *ask* me if I wanted to help you to steal from your granddad, if I wanted to join your stupid little magic circle? Oh, no, you just *drag* me along, because Trevor could never have an opinion of his own, could he? Trevor's got to be told what to do because he's too thick to decide on his own.'

'I—' Justin fished for words he couldn't find, but he didn't get a chance to speak them anyway.

'Shut *up*.' Trevor pushed him in the centre of the chest, a feeble shove but enough to throw him off-balance in his weakened state. '*I'm* talking! I have been friends with you for *eleven years*, and you have never, ever paid any attention to what *I* want. Even when there's an evil spirit in my head, you don't look at me twice! You just assume it's got to be you who's possessed, because after all, *you're* the important one. Why would Dracherion want to take over a nobody like me?'

He broke off for a moment, panting for breath.

'Well, you know what?' he said, almost tearful with rage. 'At least Dracherion never pretended that I should be *grateful* for being its slave. At least it never acted like it was doing me a favour. If it was up to me, I'd have let it kill you. I'm sorry you survived. I'm sorry *I* survived. Leave me alone.'

He stumbled off.

Justin started to take a step after him, then aborted the movement. He just watched Trevor go, completely . . . well, it was the first time he'd really understood 'gobsmacked' as a reaction. He felt like he'd just been viciously punched in the head, without any explanation or warning. Even all the things he'd seen over the past few days hadn't hit him like this, because they were just alien and amazing, not a part of the world he'd taken for granted suddenly twisting into a different shape.

Taken for granted. Justin grimaced and closed his eyes, a bitter taste rising up in his mouth.

He'd never even guessed Trevor was hiding that much resentment. Was he supposed to have seen it when it was kept so secret? Had it even been there before? He wanted to believe that the bitter tirade was some spiteful parting gift of Dracherion's, but a dull, sick feeling in the pit of his stomach told him that it wasn't. Trevor hated him, and he hadn't even noticed.

Was he really that bad? He'd thought he was *helping*. Trevor was just so nervous about everything, you had to keep really pushing to get him to do anything . . . And he never *said* when something was bothering him . . .

He'd just waited and waited for Justin to take a hint, while Justin had failed to notice there was anything wrong at all. He wondered dully whether Trevor's stewing bitterness had been just the emotional crack Dracherion had needed to force its way in and take over. Resentment and anger; exactly the sort of feelings the spirit could understand and manipulate.

Trevor's staggering silhouette left the illumination of the streetlights outside the park, and quickly melted away into the darkness.

'Well. That was predictable,' said Eilersen from behind his shoulder.

Justin wheeled round, ready to launch into ranted self-defence, but Eilersen just raised his hands.

'Hey, I'm not saying that it's your fault. Not that it *isn't*,' he added, musing. 'But as it happens, you're not *actually* the centre of the universe, so you're probably not responsible for other people's psychological problems. It was pretty obvious he was going to snap sooner or later . . . and frankly, knowing you, there's no way you could have been sensitive or insightful enough to prevent it.'

'Thank you,' Justin said sardonically, and, in a very twisted way, sort of meant it. 'I think that's the nicest thing you've ever said to me.'

There was something vaguely comforting, while the rest of the universe was losing its moorings, in discovering that Eilersen was just the same as ever.

Justin stared into the night where Trevor had disappeared, worrying at his lower lip. 'I should go after him.' The thought of finding the strength to do so, however, seemed beyond him.

Grandpa Blake rested a kindly hand on his shoulder. 'Just let him go for now,' he advised. 'Whatever his feelings, he's been through a terrible thing, and chasing after him now would be for your benefit, not his. He needs some time to come to terms with everything that's happened.'

'Yeah,' Justin said tiredly. Didn't they all.

They stood in sombre silence for a while, until he heard Joy's watch beeping the hour. He checked his own, and blinked in disbelief to see it was only nine o'clock. Surely it should be well after midnight?

His stomach felt painfully hollow, and he realized he had no idea when he'd last eaten. The day was too much of a blur to be sure if he'd stopped to eat anything at all.

Next to him, Joy yawned and gave a bone-cracking stretch. Their father eyed the pair of them with concern.

'Come on, kids. I should get you two home before you fall asleep on your feet.'

'What are we going to tell Mum?' Joy asked, rubbing her eyes. Justin hadn't even thought about that.

'Let me worry about that, huh?' said their father. 'I'll talk to your mother. Just get in the car. Dad, can I give you a lift?' For once, the offer sounded natural, not like the icy politeness he usually forced around his father.

Nonetheless, Grandpa Blake shook his head. 'I should walk,' he said, straightening up. 'There are still a few magics I need to perform when I get home, just to be on the safe side. The night air will help clear my head.'

Their father looked uncertain, and Justin couldn't blame him; it was a cold night for walking, and his grandfather was moving with noticeable stiffness. But even if the two of them had finally set aside their differences, Grandpa Blake was far too proud to accept the suggestion that he might not manage the walk.

Fortunately Eilersen stepped up to fill the awkwardness. 'I'm going that way too,' he said, very casually. 'I might as well walk back with you.'

Justin thought that perhaps Eilersen was a little bit more sensitive to the needs of other people than he liked to pretend.

He took a breath to speak, but found that the reservoir of smart comments had dried. What did you say to your schoolyard enemy when both of you had nearly died? He cleared his throat.

'So, um . . . see you around, I guess,' he said lamely.

'Probably.' Eilersen looked equally discomfited. They both just stood there for a moment, then Justin gave a jerky shrug and followed his father and sister to the car.

'How did you find us, Dad?' Joy asked as they

wearily climbed inside. 'We'd have been in trouble if you hadn't got here when you did.' The final show-down had been close, then; how close, Justin wasn't sure he wanted to know.

'Even I can put two and two together when there's a sudden resurgence of magical symbols in my life,' their father chided gently. 'I saw that the key to your grandpa's house was gone, and when you weren't back by dark, I went over there. I couldn't find you, so I just drove around until I spotted your bikes out-side the park.'

'Looks like Dracherion did us a favour there, then,' Justin observed, thinking of the slashed tyres. He wondered if that added touch had come courtesy of Trevor. A petty little act of revenge for all the petty little ways in which Justin had unknowingly made his life hell.

There was a pause, then their father twisted round in his seat so he could look at them both, Justin in the passenger side and Joy in the seat behind him. 'It should never have got this far,' he said quietly. 'What were you thinking, trying to handle something like this by yourselves?'

'Dad, it wasn't—' Joy began, but their father cut her off.

'I *know* that I have not always been . . . rational . . . about this sort of thing, but I've only ever been trying to protect you. Do you really think that's going to stop if you tell me you've done something stupid? Did you expect me to just turn around and say "I told you so"?'

Neither of them spoke. Justin kept his eyes fixed firmly on a dirty smudge at the top left of the windscreen, avoiding his father's gaze.

After a moment Dad sighed. 'However it started, and whatever you thought I was going to think, you could have come to me,' he said. 'I'm your father. How I do or don't feel about whatever kind of trouble you're in has nothing to do with it. I'm not going to walk away and leave you to get hurt just because I'm angry or disappointed.'

'We know, Dad,' Joy said softly from the back.

Justin nodded sombrely and laid his head against the cold glass of the window. They'd been lucky. More than lucky. He still didn't know what was going to happen with Trevor, and he had a feeling that, much as he'd like it to be, their brush with dark magic was still not entirely over, and might never be – but for the moment at least, Dracherion was gone, and they were all alive. Considering how incredibly stupid they'd been in so many ways, it seemed like more of a miracle than they could have asked for.

Beside him, his father plugged his seat belt in. 'We're going to talk about this,' he promised, 'but not tonight.' He heaved a slow sigh, then turned the key in the ignition and set his hands on the wheel. 'Come on, then, kids. Let's go home.'

The Devil's Footsteps

by

E. E. RICHARDSON

It was just a bit of fun, a local legend.
The Devil's Footsteps: thirteen stepping stones,
and whichever one you stopped on in the rhyme
could predict how you would die. A harmless game
for kids – and nobody ever died from a game.

But it's not a game to Bryan. He's seen the Dark
Man, because the Dark Man took his brother five years
ago. He's tried to tell himself that it was his imagination,
that the Devil's Footsteps are just stones and the Dark
Man didn't take Adam. But Adam's still gone.

And then Bryan meets two other boys who have
their own unsolved mysteries. Someone or something is
after the children in the town. And it all comes back to
the rhyme that every local child knows by heart:

Thirteen steps to the Dark Man's door,
Won't be turning back no more . . .

ISBN: 978 0 552 55171 7

The Intruders

by

E. E. RICHARDSON

If I should die before I wake,
I pray the Lord my soul to take . . .

Joel Demetrius is quite looking forward to moving in
with his new step-family, but his sister Cassie doesn't
want anything to do with Gerald and his two sons. To
make matters worse, their new home is practically derelict.

Joel is fascinated by the old house, but even he has to
admit that there's something not quite right about it.
He keeps seeing things out of the corner of his eye,
and he's plagued by nightmares of a terrified boy
who repeats the same fractured prayer over and over.

Events in the house become harder and harder to
explain, and as Cassie's battle with her stepbrothers
draws everyone deeper into the mystery, all four
kids are forced to confront the question of just
who the intruders really are . . .

ISBN: 978 0 552 552615

THE SPOOK'S APPRENTICE

by
Joseph Delaney

'The Spook's trained many, but precious few
completed their time,' Mam said, 'and those that
did aren't a patch on him. They're flawed or weak or
cowardly. They walk a twisted path taking money for
accomplishing little. So there's only you left now, son.
You're the last chance. The last hope. Someone has
to do it. Someone has to stand against the dark.
And you're the only one who can.'

Thomas Ward is the seventh son of a seventh son
and has been apprenticed to the local Spook. The job
is hard, the Spook is distant and many apprentices have
failed before him. Somehow Thomas must learn how
to exorcize ghosts, contain witches and bind boggarts.
But when he is tricked into freeing Mother Malkin, the
most evil witch in the County, the horror begins . . .

ISBN: 978 0 099 45645 2

The Hunting Season

by

DEAN VINCENT CARTER

Eight years ago the Austrian emergency
services were called to the scene of a bizarre car
accident. Eight years ago two mangled bodies were
found in the snow not far from the vehicle, clawed
and chewed by some ferocious animal. Eight years
ago something unspeakable took Gerontius Moore's
parents, leaving him orphaned and alone.
And now that something is back . . .

Caught up in a hunt he was never meant
to be a part of, and finding help from a most
unlikely source, Gerontius must once more flee
the clutches of an appalling beast, before it
learns its business is unfinished.

Full moon or not, the hunt is on!

ISBN: 978 0 552 55298 1